"Isn't she beautiful?" Meg [...]

Faye leans against the be[...] She watches me, never taking [...] and oh God, I feel her. Her l[...] [m]oves over me like furious hands. I want her to desire me. I want her to lose control, to cross the room, to grab me and push me to the bed. I want her to show Meg how it's done. I want her to drive love into me.

Her leather jacket is open. She wears nothing beneath. Her jeans are tight and her body is firm and strong. I am aroused, ready to be taken. To the place where shadows are born, that's where she'll lead me. Her hands are rough. Her cologne intoxicates. I'm caught up in her — like always, like never before.

Meg sits in a chair by the dresser. She smokes a cigarette. The fire that pierces her eyes bores into my belly . . .

With one strong hand, Faye keeps my arms raised high above my head. She plucks one nipple. We both watch as it blooms into a thickened maroon rectangle. She tugs it again. I'm drenched with wicked anticipation. Will she fuck me? Will she have me? Will she show Meg, will she show me, exactly how bad I've been?

~IN THE MOOD~

ROBBI SOMMERS

THE NAIAD PRESS, INC.
1997

Printed in the United States of America on acid-free paper
First Edition

Editor: Christine Cassidy
Cover designer: Bonnie Liss (Phoenix Graphics)
Typesetter: Sandi Stancil

Library of Congress Cataloging-in-Publication Data

Sommers, Robbi, 1950 –
  In the mood / by Robbi Sommers.
      p.   cm.
  ISBN 1-56280-172-4 (pbk.)
  1. Lesbians—Fiction. I. Title.
PS3569.065335I5   1997
813'.54—dc21   97-10808
                                                         CIP

JE NE REGRETTE RIEN

For my muse...

About the Author

Besides her best-selling lesbian erotica, Robbi Sommers' work (fiction, nonfiction and poetry) has been published in various magazines and anthologies including *Redbook, Reader's Digest* and *Penthouse*.

BOOKS BY ROBBI SOMMERS

CONTENTS

Cheers to the Bus Driver

I swerved into the parking lot and cut the ignition. Eight twenty-five. I debated taking an Extra Strength Excedrin before the inevitable headache began. Once again, Alex had roped me into something. Once again, I was embarking on an escapade just because she'd asked. Why did I still fall victim to her every whim? After all, *she* broke up with *me*. Her life is full and exciting.

Me? I work, come home and then mope. It aggravates me that she flits around town like a carefree dragonfly while I move through life like a snail. Nonetheless, when Alex calls, when she pleads with me in that sensuous butch tone of hers, it's hard to refuse her anything.

Alex knows she has me on a moment's notice. She starts with that smooth voice and I'm hers. So when she asked me to surrender my first day off in weeks to accompany her son on a second-grade field trip, there was really no question whether I'd succumb. "I have to work," she had pouted. "Casey will be *so* disappointed," her tone slippery wet.

I'm Jewish. The idea of a bumpy hour ride to the ferry (car sickness?), a choppy half-hour cruise to Angel Island (sea sickness?), a two-hour trek up a hill (dizziness? leg cramps? poison oak?) was not a pretty one. This was not what my people consider a good time...

Eight twenty-seven. I downed two Dramamine, dropped a couple Excedrin in my pocket, climbed out of the car and headed across the street. Casey's class was already lining up by the yellow bus when I came around the building.

"Aunt Gaile!" Casey broke out of line. "My aunt's here! My aunt's here!"

"Hey, Casey." I swallowed him in a hug.

"Good morning, I'm Angela Nystrom — Casey's teacher." She offered me a glad-you-could-make-it smile. "And this is Betsy Braxton, the other field trip parent."

"Hi. I'm Sissy's mom." Betsy shook my hand.

2

A typical heterosexual mother — her acorn-colored hair curled in a perfect pageboy, her lipstick sugar-sweet pink. "Looks like we're the only parents that could make it today." She smiled sympathetically.

"I'm Gaile Schusterman, Casey's aunt."

"Any questions before we start?" Angela reviewed a roster of names.

Why couldn't little Sissy have a big butch mom? That's the only question I really cared about. "How's this going to work?" I asked instead.

"Once we get to the ferry, we'll split into three groups. Eight students each. The ride will be around forty-five minutes."

"My aunt and me are goin' to sit right up front. Right, Aunt Gaile? Can we?"

I glanced at the school bus. I hadn't even considered seating logistics. Ride in the back of a school bus as it curved and swayed to our destination? The mere thought of it sent a wave of nausea through me.

"Better hurry then, honey." I gave him a little nudge. All I could think about was getting on the bus and grabbing a front seat. Even if I had to push a couple kids out of our way, Casey and I would sit up front. Period. I grabbed Casey's hand and gave Ms. Nystrom and Betsy a here-goes smile. "See you on board."

* * * * *

3

Three kids had squeezed into the seat behind the driver's. The adjacent front seat was occupied by a freckle-faced boy who sat squarely in the middle. There was barely enough room for me, let alone Casey. As far as I was concerned, the kid was in the wrong seat.

"I need you to move back a seat," I said sweetly.

"I was here first," he muttered. Stubbornness dripped from his words.

I studied his name tag. Jimmy. Jimmy with the belligerent expression plastered across his too-cute-to-like face. Wasn't I bigger? Didn't kids have to listen when the field trip parent gave direction? The urge to yank him from the seat and plant him elsewhere was strong.

"Now, Jimmy —" I kept my voice surprisingly even. "You know a parent needs to sit up front, don't you? That's the rule." One advantage of being "the adult" is the liberty to invent rules as needed.

He shook his head obstinately.

I grit my teeth. "You know that rule. I know you do."

He crossed his arms against his chest and peered straight ahead. Behind me, pushing against me, kids filtered onto the bus. Time was dwindling. Options were narrowing. If I didn't handle this quickly, I'd end up in the back for sure. The image of me hanging from the back window, dry-heaving as the bus wove down the freeway, was ugly.

"Let's all cooperate, Jimmy." A sing-song lilt lifted my voice.

He recrossed his arms and shook his head again.

"Jimmy." I lowered my tone to bully level. No response. The bus was full except three seats in the very back. No fucking way. "Okay, fine," I snapped. "Casey, push in with Jimmy. We're all going to share."

"Yea, front seat!" Casey cheered. He nudged against Jimmy who reluctantly slid toward the window. I plopped in beside Casey. Crammed in the seat, one-quarter of my butt hanging into the aisle — this was not a good start. Weary already, I closed my eyes. Was every eight-year-old on the bus hollering? I desperately fingered the Excedrin in my pocket.

"Okay, everyone, listen up." A woman's voice cruised over the clamor. "There are a few rules I need to go over." The shouting continued. "I said, listen up!"

A labored silence descended through the bus. Eyes still closed, breathing slow and easy, I practiced my buddy Marlene's deep relaxation technique. This was going to be one hell of a long trip.

"Kids have to stay seated. I mean it." She had a tough tone. Good. Any more shit from Jimmy and I'd call in allies. "Windows stay up. No screaming. Got that?"

The bus was amazingly quiet.

"If there's an emergency and for some reason I can no longer drive the bus, the front seat parent will —"

The front-seat parent? I immediately peeked at the adjacent front seat. Nope. No parent there. Just me. I was the only front-seat parent. My body stiffened. I gulped air. *The front-seat parent will what?* I couldn't be involved in emergency procedures. I'm a femme. A *Jewish* femme. My job is to run for help. A thick panic smothered me. *The front-seat parent will what?* I'll plead for mercy, fake a limp, act erratic . . .

Hoping to somehow diffuse the situation, I shot a fast look at the bus driver. It was in that moment, that simple, solitary moment, that the rock-hard dynamics of the field trip melted away. Not only was the driver very, very attractive, but she appeared to be — and God knows I'm usually right on the money when it comes to this — a deliciously butch dyke.

Her black hair was close-cropped in a boy-cut. About five-seven with a strong, stocky build, she had one hand on her hip, the other pushed in her pants pocket. Her snug jeans emphasized her full hips and muscular thighs. My focus lingered momentarily then slid to the scuffed army boots

6

she wore. Her sleeveless, button-down shirt revealed sculptured biceps, tapering forearms, capable hands — hands that could control a bus with the slightest twist of a finger. Thick fingers, fast fingers.

"— need to stop the bus by pulling this lever."

I returned my attention to her face. She was staring at me — *the front-seat parent* — the front-seat parent who on this day, in this seat, looked like anybody's heterosexual mom. Just another Betsy Braxton riding in a bus.

I shifted in the seat. Maybe she'd catch a glimpse of the gay pride pin on my jacket? *I'm one of you,* I thought over and over, just in case all the information in the psychic books Marlene had been reading actually worked. *I'm a dyke. I'm a dyke. I'm a dyke.*

"This will connect you with the dispatcher." Still peering at me, she pointed to a radio on the dashboard. "Just press right here and talk."

I'll press there if you'll press here. I squeezed my thighs tightly together and a slight pleasure radiated between my legs. I sat up straight and flipped my hair behind my back. See the pin? See?

Maybe she'd already noticed the pin! Maybe that's why she'd singled me out. I smiled. *I'm a femme. See?* I batted my eyes. *I'm a dyke. I'm one of you.* Dyke energy always seems to seek and find its own. It's one of those rarely discussed principles of physics. I recognized her . . . she recognized me . . . Pull the lever? Sure. Radio for help? No problem. The front-seat parent was ready to assist.

Our eyes locked. A thousand words traveled between us. *You chose me because this was your way of flirting, right?* I smiled.

How could I not want you to pull the lever? Her lips hadn't moved, but I heard each word.

Her gaze broke from me and soared to the rest of the bus. "Any questions?"

The silence in the bus broke into laughs and shouts. The driver slid into her seat and started the bus. Had she glanced at me in her overhead mirror? Of course she had. Simple physics — like seeks like. I smiled. The bus rumbled and we began to roll.

The all-American heterosexual Betsy suggested a group round of "Cheers to the Bus Driver." Little Jimmy crossed his arms and refused to sing. But in my opinion, Betsy had a point. *Cheers to the bus driver with us today.*

The driver acted as if she was concentrating intently on the road ahead, but she couldn't hide her desire, not from me. Each time her focus shifted to the rear-view mirror, I felt a wave of heat drift toward my seat. Each time she glanced in the side mirror, I knew it was me she was trying to see.

I centered my attention on the overhead mirror. When she scanned the back of the bus, I could see her eyes. I waited for them to connect with mine. What a tease she was! Not once acknowledging me. What a flirt! Didn't matter. Wasn't *I* the front-seat parent? Hadn't she singled me out? It doesn't get much clearer than that. Still waters run deep.

I fished for the tube of lipstick in my jacket pocket. She was so obviously butch. So predictably butch. Easy to entrance, easy to maneuver. I restrained a giggle. A hint of red lipstick brings women like her to their knees.

The lipstick smeared easily onto my fingertip. With an experienced flair, I dabbed it on my lips. I shifted slightly, determined to catch her eye in the overhead mirror.

"I have to pee." Jimmy had reached over Casey and was tapping my arm.

"Not now, Jimmy," I muttered without glancing at him. I was busy.

"Gotta pee *now*."

"Jimmy has to pee . . . Jimmy has to pee," Casey sang.

Jimmy elbowed Casey. Casey pushed Jimmy.

"Cool it. Just cool it." The words pushed hard under my breath. "We *do not* humiliate the front-seat parent."

"What's humiliate?" Casey asked loudly.

"Got to pee, now," Jimmy demanded.

"Okay. Okay. Okay." I shot him a dirty look.

"I have to pee, too," the girl across the aisle whispered.

Jesus Christ. Who even had time to get car sick? I peered down the aisle. Now what? Ms. Nystrom was way in the back. Did I risk that long, unsteady walk down the aisle? I figured the nausea would hit around row eight. I'd collapse at fourteen. I'd look like a fool. A ridiculous fool.

"Problem?" The driver glanced at me from the overhead mirror.

I grabbed onto the pole and pulled myself out of the seat. For some reason the walk to her seemed smooth and steady. Two steps and I was at her side. The bus tried its best to toss me to the floor but I held my ground and leaned in close.

"They have to pee." I gestured to the kids behind me, all the while praying that an unexpected bump would send me stumbling into her lap.

"They'll have to wait."

Was this woman butch or what! Talking in that top tone of hers. Setting things straight. *They'll have to wait.* Life poses no difficulties when there's a butch in charge.

I turned toward Jimmy. "Sorry, honey," I cooed. "The bus driver says we'll have to wait."

Back to the driver — surely she'd seen my pin
by now — I debated my next move. *Some ride,
huh? You like this kind of work? Come here often?*
"You'll need to be seated." Her tone was
clipped.

Hadn't she seen my pin? As if I'd lost my
balance, I held onto the pole and swung toward
her. No way she'd miss the gay pride pin now.
I'm a dyke. I'm a dyke. I'm a dyke. "Whoa, rough
ride!"

"That's why you have to stay seated."

The cold shoulder. Disheartened, I staggered
back to my seat. How far did a woman have to
push things to get somewhere? In a second, Alex
would have had this driver eating out of her
hand. *That's why you have to stay seated.* The
words reverberated bitterly. I was a snail, a snail,
a snail.

"Gotta pee," Jimmy insisted.

"Tell it to the driver, Jim." I cut his name
short. After all, hadn't we all aged in the past ten
minutes?

An accident in San Rafael brought traffic to a
standstill. By the time we reached the pier, the
ferry was halfway to Angel Island.

"Next ferry's at eleven forty-five." Ms. Nystrom had already been off and on the bus three times working out an alternative plan.

I sat in the front seat, face cradled in my hands. The idea of keeping tabs on a group of eight-year-olds as they raced on the water's edge made me dizzy. I would never, ever let Alex rope me into another thing.

I peeked through my fingers. Ms. Nystrom was at the head of the bus. "We're going to have to be flexible —" She paused, scanning the crowded bus. "We can be flexible, can't we, children? We'll do a walking tour of Tiburon, eat our lunches at the park and then ride to Angel Island."

"Can we leave our purses on the bus?" Betsy called from the middle of the bus.

Ms. Nystrom looked to the driver who'd climbed out of her seat.

"Feel free to leave whatever you want. I'll be here with the bus the whole time you're gone." She glanced at me and smiled.

Was that a signal? Her way of telling me to try to come back? Nonchalantly, I took off my jacket and discreetly kicked it beneath my seat.

The kids poured out of the bus and within seconds had located the town candy store. Smearing the window, knocking on the glass, the kids were in some sort of a frenzy. "Can we go in there? Can we get some candy?"

I managed to pry my group away from the

scene and lead them to the restroom. From the restroom, through the town, they ran and I followed. We met up with the others in the park at eleven.

When we'd settled down for lunch, I temporarily turned my group over to Ms. Nystrom and headed back to the bus. *Left my jacket. Be right back.*

As if the driver was expecting a discreet liaison, she'd parked the bus beneath a grove of trees at the far end of the parking lot. She sat in the driver's seat, her face buried in a book.

I gave a quick knock on the door. "I think I left my jacket on board."

Her attention shifted to me. "Oh yeah?"

"Yeah." I climbed the first step into the bus. "Front seat."

Step. Step. I was next to her.

She closed the book, got out of her seat and stood so close that I almost stumbled backwards, out of the bus.

"It's not up front . . ." She looked me straight in the eye. "Ma'am."

Was that flirting? But the *ma'am*. The *ma'am* was the key. As far as she was concerned, I was just another straight mom. A husband-at-home, uninterested-in-a-beautiful-butch wife. Another one of the thousand Betsy Braxtons she must see every week.

"I was sitting right there." Not moving, I gestured toward the seat.

"It's not up front." She glanced at the gay pride pin (didn't she?) and smiled. "It's in the back. The lost and found."

Oh, so that was her game. She'd get me to the back of the bus and then make her move.

For a brief moment I fell into a fantasy . . .

"I couldn't help noticing you," she'd say.

"Really? I didn't think you'd even seen me." I'd bat my eyes. Lick my lips.

"Not notice a beautiful woman like you? Impossible."

She'd take my hand and lead me to the back of the bus . . .

I peeked at the driver. I was *not* just another mother. I was *not* just another Betsy hurry-home-to-hubby Braxton. Couldn't she see? I was a dyke. A lipstick femme, yes, but a dyke all the same.

The lost and found, in the back. Would she escort me there? Was that the plan? I gave the driver a subtle once-over. Well?

We'd get to the back of the bus and she'd squat on the floor. "The lost and found is down here."

I'd squat next to her. I'd lean real close. My *Chanel No. 5,* my flirty smile, my hand lightly brushing against hers . . .

"What a clever place for a lost and found!" I'd say. Butches love to be complimented on their ingenuity.

14

"Think so?" She'd be pleased that I noticed.

"Oh yes." I'd bat my eyes for good measure. "I've been on some buses ... well, you can't even begin to imagine the lost-and-found nightmares I could tell you about ... but this ... the way this wooden box fits right under the seat ... did you make it?"

She'd smile. "I'm a cabinet maker when I'm not driving a bus."

"Oh really! How ambitious!" She'd love that — the admiration, the interest.

She'd be uncertain at first, but finally, she'd get up the nerve and kiss me. Kiss me and kiss me and kiss me.

I'd kiss her back like she'd never been kissed before.

She'd touch my face. Pull me close — her lips on my mouth. Warm. Wet. Her hands on my breasts.

"Let me." I'd unbutton my blouse. "Let me." I'd unzip my pants. All I'd want is her fingers. All I'd want is her fingers pushing past the lace of my panties, ripping at the lace of my panties, plunging beneath the lace of my panties.

"Let me!" I'd mutter and pull down my pants. "Let me," I'd gasp and lie down in the aisle.

She'd know what I'd want. She's a butch. Clever and ingenious and ambitious and fast. She'd know what I'd want and kiss me, kiss me, kiss me, kiss me.

Her mouth on mine is sugar. Her mouth is

sticky heat. I melt. I soften into putty. I think of the weight of her body. The strength of her hands. Her biceps. Her triceps. Her dark hair. Her smile.

She'd climb on top, her hands sliding across my belly, her perfume a swirl of cinnamon, patchouli, orange and spice. She'd slowly move her hips. Kissing me again and again. Finally, her fingers would delve further and further into my heat. Into my slick damp.

I would be hers. I would simply be hers. Whatever she wanted. Whatever she did . . . hers, hers, hers.

Her fingers are thick. Her fingers are hungry for me. Down and down. I'm squirming. I'm pleading for more.

"There." She slips a finger into me. "There," she mutters again. She works her finger against my clit. I'm hard. I'm on fire. Back and forth, back and forth, her finger greases its way over my rigid flesh. I'm riding up and down in the back of the bus. I'm spinning in circles in the back of the bus.

Dizzy, I don't care. Bouncing up and down, I don't care.

Her mouth on my breast. Her mouth on my neck. My ear. My cheek. Over and over, all she says is "There. There. There."

I grab her hair.

We have to be fast.

I bite her neck.

We have to be fast.

I arch to meet her.

Fast.

"There. There," she mumbles again and again . . .

"You see it?" The bus driver pointed toward the back of the bus. "On that pile." She plopped back in her seat and picked up the book.

That was it? A point and a nod?

Surely, if she knew I was a lesbian, if she knew I was interested, if she knew that I wanted her mouth on mine, she'd be more sociable. "I —"

The bus driver glanced at me. "Huh?"

"I just wondered if you knew —"

"Problem here?" Betsy wife-of-the-year Braxton stepped into the bus.

"Oh . . . I . . . I . . . was just heading to the lost and found . . . see . . . right there, back of the bus . . . oh, and there . . . there's my jacket . . . right on top." I hurried down the aisle, grabbed the jacket and leapt from the bus.

"Oh and look! There's *my* jacket, too," I heard Betsy say to the driver. A sarcastic edge in her voice.

I hurried across the lot, turned the corner and headed for the group of kids. But then — call it one of Marlene's "intuitions" — I stopped, turned and peeked around the corner.

The bus door was closed. Betsy and the driver stood in the back. Betsy laughed, did a quick glance around the lot and then lightly touched the driver's cheek.

The ride home was miserable. The road seemed windier, the bus stuffy and the urge to dry-heave taunted me every inch of the way. And when cheery Betsy Braxton merrily got the group to break into another round of "Cheers to the Bus Driver" — little Jimmy and I crossed our arms and refused to sing along.

Marie

Okay, yes, I admit it. I paid for sex: paid for the drinks, paid for the room and then, paid for the woman. One hundred and seventy-five an hour.

A personal ad led me to her. The words — simple and to the point — caught my attention and wouldn't let go. *Escorts. Women for women. Discreet.* I meant to turn the page, to continue my search for Ann Landers' column but instead found myself staring absently at the tiny, black-bordered ad.

Hire a woman? I laughed at the absurdity. *Hire a woman?* What woman would! And yet, I couldn't seem to pull my focus from those five unembellished words. What harm in calling the number, just to see, just to have a feel for how these things work? Not that I would ever consider, not that I would have an interest...

I expected a sleazy answering machine message. Quick eavesdrop into the life and fantasies of someone else, and then I'd hang up. But before I knew what had hit me, I was caught in the middle of a sex-for-hire transaction. Someone had answered the line. Someone wanted to know when, where and what, specifically, I wanted.

"I want her to wear a suit and tie." *I do?* My mind was racing. *I do?* The drop in my belly was reminiscent of a roller coaster ride. The slamming of my heart drowned out my feeble words. Requirements seemed to be spilling from me. What was I doing? Why couldn't I slow this exchange down? "And she should be taller than me, five-six, five-seven, with long, tied-back hair." Oh shit, I was out of control!

I should have hung up. I should have tossed that portable phone across the room and moved directly to Ann Landers, but I didn't. I held fast that receiver like a kid does a balloon on a windy day and muttered my demands.

"Older," I insisted. "Classy." After all, for three hundred and fifty hard-earned dollars . . . Yes. Two hours. Yes. I'd have cash.

"The Fairmount?" she suggested.

"Yes. Perfect," I replied. How surprisingly easy this was! "In the lobby, Friday night at eight."

I placed the phone on the table. I stared at the black-edged ad. *Friday night at eight?* Had I actually consented? Did I really think I'd go to the Fairmount and take some woman up to a room and . . . and . . . *And what?*

The transaction whirled around me like a hurricane. Two hours. Three hundred and fifty dollars. Oh my God.

I sat in the lobby of the Fairmount Hotel like a reluctant patient in a dentist's chair. How I had gotten here, I couldn't be sure. I'd merely buy her a drink, small talk for a bit, and then get the hell out of there as soon as I could. Even so, four one-hundred dollar bills were crammed in my coat pocket. Not that I would actually go through with this scheme. Not that I would end up in bed with a woman for hire — but who could have guessed that I'd even be in a hotel lobby, waiting for a one-hundred-seventy-five-dollar-an-hour date?

My heart thumped recklessly. My slinky black dress hiked slightly up my thigh. Had I not painted my lips in ruby red? Had I not trailed a wet line of perfume between my full breasts, across my sloped belly and into the soft tangle of sex hair? Life being what it was, circumstances twisting as they do, it was always best to be prepared on the off chance that —

On the off chance that what? The sudden urge to hurry out of the hotel, climb into my car and screech out of the parking lot overwhelmed me. What was I thinking? Dressed in black garters and lace —— what the hell was I thinking? I reached for my keys, rose from the chair and —

"Excuse me?" The voice gushed through me like liquid heat. "I thought perhaps you were waiting for me?"

I froze. The sound of rushing blood swished in my ears. *Turn around,* something inside me insisted. *Turn around and smile.* In a long, slow movement that seemed to last an eternity, I pivoted. And there she stood. Five-six? Five-seven? It was difficult to be sure, what with the distraction of her kohl-lined eyes, what with the allure of her cherry-red lips.

"Are you Marie?" My voice cracked.

She nodded and extended her hand. A sparkle of fiery red glittered from a thin gold ring that decorated her index finger. If I took her hand in mine, then what? If I lightly ran my fingertip across that jeweled band, then what? My palms felt clammy. A harsh hollowness ballooned in my chest. *Take her hand.*

"Nice to meet you." Her hand was warm, soft, satiny.

In the lobby of the Fairmount, her hand in mine, I stood immobilized. *Now what the hell did I do?* My gaze slid from her Egyptian-shadowed eyes and lingered on those voluptuous lips.

"Do you have a room?" She squeezed my hand lightly and then slipped hers from mine.

I felt the sudden lack of her softness and wrestled with the urge to grab her hand and hold it roughly. After all, wasn't this my party? Didn't I call the shots? Yes, I had a room. Yes, I had four hundred dollars in my jacket and yes, yes, yes, I could grasp her hand if that's what I wanted — or could I? The car was through the doors and in the garage. I could be out of here and safe in three fast breaths. *Did I have a room?* And what? We go up there? We take off our clothes? How the hell had I gotten into this situation?

Once again, she took my hand. I felt abruptly transported out of my hesitations and into the steamy sensation of her touch. One moment we were in the lobby, the next we were sitting in my room sipping champagne. Had we had a conversation? How much time had already passed? Lost in a golden champagne haze, I concentrated on the sparkle of her diamond earrings.

"You're very attractive." She rose from her

chair and let her suit jacket drop to the floor. "When I came into the lobby, I hoped you were the one."

Slowly, deliberately, she unknotted her tie and pulled it from around her neck. Her silk shirt, secured with small pearl buttons, opened with ease. Beneath, she wore exquisite lace lingerie. Her black bra barely contained her tempting breasts and the arc of her brown areolas spilled above the low demi-cups. I had an immediate hunger to see more. Were her nipples large and square? Small and pointy? Would their brick-red color contrast with her olive skin? Or were they pale? Or pink? Or a deep, deep plum?

I leaned forward. I was breathing hard and my mouth felt sucked dry. Would she unhook the bra? Would she show me what she had?

"Marie." Had I spoken or was her name ricocheting inside my mind? "Marie, Marie, Marie."

She ran her hands across the black lace. And yes, oh yes, she released the bra's silver hook. Thicker than I could have dreamed, larger than I could have hoped, her nipples stood out like fat cherry pits. I felt suddenly dizzy. A creamy aching throbbed between my legs.

Marie, Marie, Marie.

She plucked a nipple between her fingers and twisted and tugged.

"Marie," I whispered. "Marie," I begged.

She unzipped her pants and they crumpled to the floor. Her bikini panties rose high on the delicious curve of her hips. She stepped out of her shoes and sat on the edge of the bed.

"Would you like to see all of me?" She separated her legs and ran her finger along the lace border of the panties. A dark fringe of hair teased from beneath the lace. The panties stretched tight over the thick bulge of her lips and I was certain her sex would be bulky and lush. And yes, yes, yes, I wanted, needed, had to see it all.

Her fingertip grazed the center point of her crotch. It was difficult to be certain, but the material seemed to be wet. If she pulled those panties aside, would her moisture glisten in the light? Should I move closer? Fall on my knees at her feet, rip those panties aside and see for myself?

I imagined her — a ruby in pillowy folds. If she'd move those panties aside and spread open her lips, I could know for sure. The fragrance of sex hung heavy in the air. Entrancing musk blended with an intoxicating spice into a primal, raw scent. All I could think of was her pussy. All I could consider was the color of that ruby buried like a treasure behind the lace veil of her panties.

Like a desperate baby, I crawled across the floor for the honey and sweet. Marie was laughing. The room was spinning. *Marie. Marie.*

Marie. I yanked those panties aside, pulled that flimsy lace out of my way and buried my face in her soft charms.

She was slippery heat. Submerged in dark desire, I found her with my mouth and sucked, sucked, sucked. She was all over me. She reached down and cleaved her lips open. Ravenous to see more, I pulled back. Her clit sac dangled like a dark pink ornament. I licked it once, lapped it again. *Marie, Marie, Marie.* The lower lips parted like rose curtains. Wanting more, needing more, I grabbed them between my fingers and split them wide, exposing her swollen entrance.

Sex juice shimmered on the raised rim. I dipped my finger in, stirred, pierced the soft indentation.

Marie was squirming, grinding her hips. I burrowed into the velvet pie. Her clit strained forward. Her lips wrapped around the base of my finger and her pussy clamped hard.

I jammed my other hand under my dress and into my dampness. As I fucked her, I flicked my finger across my clit. I was hard. I was oversized. I was warm and oily. In and out, I pumped my finger into her. Back and forth, I whipped my finger across my clit. Again and again, over and over.

Engulfed in pinks and reds, surrounded in the hot perfume of lust, I spun in a vortex of pleasure. It was dark. It was light. I was swimming in slippery gels, floating on a sun-baked lake, swirling in a tropical storm. The slapping sounds as I pounded into her lifted me high in the air. Again and again, more and more. *Marie, Marie, Marie.*

Okay, yes, I admit it. I paid for sex: paid for the drinks, paid for the room and then, paid for the woman. Not that I would ever consider, not that I would have an interest . . . but the following week, when I called the escort service just to say thanks, a disconnect notice was all I got.

Rational curiosity, and nothing more, compelled me to hire the private investigator. Marie. Marie. Marie. Where are you, Marie?

Waiting for Faye

I'm uncertain how much more of Faye's "need to be free" I can take. To distract myself, I've started seeing Meg. I like Meg's power. I like how she tops me. I like that her desire is interwoven with a fierce underlying need. Even so, I have fugitive fantasies about Faye. My addiction to her hounds me. I dial her number and hang up the moment she picks up the phone. In a peculiar way, it releases the pressure not seeing her creates.

Meg helps me dodge the pain, but still, I'm a victim of the dark, sharp passion that missing Faye brings. Will Faye come back to me once again? Will she wake up one day and realize that it's been too long — that she should have called me over three months ago?

This time the breakup has been different. In the past, after a month, no more than two, Faye always called. "I miss you," she'd murmur. "I've made a mistake." The anticipation of Faye's return is usually enough to soothe me. I wait for the moment she slips from cool to warm, from gone to here. But this time, she's disappeared. No call. No whisper in my ear, no Faye.

Where is she?

I'm lonely and sad and sleeping with Meg.

The truth is, I want nothing from anyone but Faye. I stare at the phone and wait for her to call. I read old letters she sent, I listen to the music she likes to hear. Lately, I've gone one step further. I dial her number and listen. "Hello?" The sound of Faye's cool voice sends a thrill through me. I sit in a dark room and simply listen to her voice. "Hello? Hello?"

She knows who's calling, I have no doubt . . . yet she never says my name. Is this her idea of a game? A clever ploy to make me want her even more? Perhaps she doesn't understand the depth of my hunger for her — I'm starving.

Starved.

Ravenous.

I call her and hang up — once, twice, sometimes three times day. My need for her is insatiable.

I light a cigarette and stare at the phone. Should I call her again? *Hello? Hello?*

Nine P.M. Ten.

Ten-fifteen, the phone rings.

Faye? I lunge for the receiver. "Yes?"

"I've got a present for you." It's Meg. Her voice is thick and syrupy. "It's something special. Something you'll never forget. After all, your birthday is Friday."

The disappointment lingers only momentarily. Meg knows how to anesthetize me with sexual innuendoes. Her repertoire is vast and time spent with her dulls my chronic ache.

The phone seems suddenly warm against my ear. The hurt thins to a slender black line.

"I'm thinking about your ex. A private birthday party with just the three of us. She fucks you and I watch. Wouldn't that be the best present for the sweetest girl?"

"My ex?" I say cautiously. Does she mean Faye? A private party with Faye? Impossible. Faye would never agree. Faye does things her way, and her way only. Faye would slam down the phone if Meg called, would turn the other cheek if Meg approached her. This was a trick. Some kind of a trick. An impossible, nasty trick.

"Who . . . ?" I mutter. Perhaps I'm mistaken. Maybe she means someone else. Someone from before Faye?

"Oh please," Meg interrupts. "There's only one ex who really counts."

Is this a test? A way for Meg to find out how I really feel about Faye? Whenever she's asked, I've denied any attachment to Faye. After all, it really isn't Meg's business, is it?

"I'm not certain who —"

"Oh I see, you want to play naïve, huh? C'mon, Lea — no need. Anyway, it's already been arranged. Faye said yes."

My heart starts thumping. *Faye said yes? Faye said yes?*

"I want to watch her fuck you," Meg says. My heart pounds so loudly that I'm unsure if she's still speaking. "I know the power Faye has over you." Her words crash in between thunderous heartbeats. "Shit. Everyone knows. She walks out, a month later she snaps her fingers and you come running. But it looks like she's not coming back this time . . ."

Looks like she's not coming back this time. How would Meg know? How would anyone know? Faye is unpredictable. Faye has her reasons.

"So as a treat, I've decided to give you something special."

Something special.

Something special.

Something special.

I close my eyes and see Faye in my bedroom. The only light comes from candles. Candles everywhere. Dressed in black. Sleek in black, I'd wear something sexy. Lace and leather and patent leather high heels. I'd dance for her. I'd slither like a snake. I'd grind my hips, seductive and slow. I know how she likes it. I know what she needs . . .

"Isn't she beautiful?" Meg says.

Faye leans against the bedroom door, silent. She watches me, never taking her eyes from me — and oh God, I feel her. Her lust moves over me like furious hands. I want her to desire me. I want her to lose control, to cross the room, to grab me and push me to the bed. I want her to show Meg how it's done. I want her to drive love into me.

Her leather jacket is open. She wears nothing beneath. Her jeans are tight and her body is firm and strong. I am aroused, ready to be taken. To the place where shadows are born, that's where she'll lead me. Her hands are rough. Her cologne intoxicates. I'm caught up in her — like always, like never before.

Meg sits in a chair by the dresser. She smokes a cigarette. The fire that pierces her eyes bores into my belly.

A heavy ache pulls at my clit. Love and desire, hurt and need, all tangle into a knot. I dance to the music. I am sexy. I am free. Nothing can harm me now. I close my eyes; it doesn't matter, my flesh burns.

Faye crosses the room. Her desire has me wild and ready. When she takes me, it will be hard and forceful. I know this. I know how I call forth her dark side.

I am wet. I am slippery. I unhook my bra and let it drop to the floor. My nipples are red bullets. My belly slopes. My hips curve. I have trimmed my sex hair and my little lips hang sweetly in view. I dance the dark. I conjure magic to sidestep a relationship that makes me cry. The fact that Faye deserted me several months before disappears like a fleeting silhouette. I am hot. Hot and ready.

Faye grabs my wrists. She pulls my hands above my head. I feel my dampness seeping. I am so ready.

"You see this, Meg?" she says. "Do you see what a bad girl she is?"

She talks to me like I'm a little girl and the suggestion that I'll finally be taken care of pours over me like hot honey. She lets me know that she controls the situation and at last, I can let go. I

34

hunger for the freedom of being her girl once again.

"A bad, bad girl," Meg says smoothly. She takes a drag on her cigarette.

"Daddy knows just how bad you've been," Faye continues. "But Meg doesn't know, not really." She laughs. "Calling me and hanging up. Each day. Every day."

With one strong hand, Faye keeps my arms raised high above my head. She plucks one nipple. We both watch as it blooms into a thickened maroon rectangle. She tugs it again. I'm drenched with wicked anticipation. Will she fuck me? Will she have me? Will she show Meg, will she show me, exactly how bad I've been?

Her hands travel over my belly to my trimmed pussy. She teases me, running her fingertips along the perimeter of the dark triangle. Then, in a fast move, she yanks me to the bed and pushes me down. She's angry. She's angry that I'm no longer hers, that I'm here because of Meg's genius.

I like her roughness. I like her fury. I like to know exactly what is what. She spreads my legs and in seconds is on her knees at the edge of the bed. Meg says nothing. She draws from the cigarette in long, low breaths. I imagine her eyes are blazing. After all, by now, she's probably angry, too.

Faye slips her fingers into the wet of my cunt. I am ready. I want it all. She pulls me apart and then sucks and nibbles my tiny clit. The room is filled with the sound of her hunger. She's light. She's direct. She finds my hard center and laps me good. I want to scream. I want to make her see how I crave love.

Faye's fingers probe along the rim of my entrance. It is good. It is so good that I want to cry. I want to cry for every moment I've felt alone. I want to cry for every second I've thought I wasn't enough or thought I was too much. I am exhausted from dodging love's hollow-tipped bullets.

Meg stands up. She steps closer. I don't blame her. I'd step closer, too. Faye is plugging a finger into my slit. Her fingers search, they explore, she's looking for soul somewhere down there. So am I. So am I.

She starts to fuck me slow and easy. I've escaped to a place where I can't be touched. I've retreated to a place where I'm invincible. After all, Faye loves me.

Faye pulls all her power into herself and then takes me with one swift stroke. Oh dear, dear God. Oh, dear God. I am hers. I am hers. I am safe and sweet and okay. In this moment I am hers, hers, hers. No one can touch me now. I'm on the ceiling, I'm on the roof, I'm riding the clouds where I can't be found.

"She's so sweet." Faye turns to Meg. "Isn't she? Isn't she?"

I want to cry.

I am so sweet, aren't I?

* * * * *

"I know the power Faye has over you. I want to see you succumb to that," Meg says again and I crash back into reality. I'm grasping the phone. Meg's voice is a low buzz.

"I can't believe Faye agreed," I mumble, thinking maybe if Meg called Faye it will jar her, bring her back to me.

"Faye's in the palm of my hand," she says, smartass that she is, and she slams down the phone.

After Meg's call, it's hard to control myself. I want to dial Faye's number again. I want to hear her voice. Why does she do this to me? Every three months she starts a fight, walks out and doesn't return for a month or two . . . it's been longer this time. Why has she waited so long? *Looks like she's not coming back this time.* Is that what she told Meg? Maybe Meg's call will jar her? Maybe once she knows I have a lover, Faye will come back to me.

The phone rings. I peer at the clock. Eleven-thirty P.M.

Faye?

"Yes?" I whisper into the phone.

"I've got you, Lea." Meg's voice is white heat. "I've got you now."

"Oh yeah?" I lean back in my bed, close my eyes and wait for the numbing to begin.

"I just spoke with *her.*"

I act nonchalant but my body is tight. "Her?"

"Yeah, your favorite ex." Meg doesn't hide the edge in her voice. "I said, 'Our little girl's agreed to the party, Faye.' " Meg laughs. *"Our little girl. You like the way that sounds, Lea? Our little girl?"* Meg starts laughing and doesn't stop.

Sometimes I think Meg is crazy.

I'm caught off guard when Faye calls. Not even a hello, not even a mention of the flurry of hang-up calls. "Did you give *her* my phone number?" is all she says.

I spiral in a vortex of desire and anxiety.

"Her?" I said. "Her?" I breathe. I take a moment to calm the spinning sensation. *Faye. Faye. Faye.* "What are you talking about?" My voice sounds innocent but flat.

"You know goddamn well who." Anger spills through Faye's words. "Your new girlfriend, Meg."

"Meg?" I say carefully. "I wouldn't call Meg a girlfriend —"

"Yeah, right." Faye interrupts.

"Meg called you?" I keep my voice even. I feel weak inside. Will she say she wants to see me? That she's ready to come home?

"She called about your birthday. About having a little party."

"I don't know what you're talking about." What is it about Faye that compels me to lie? My heart pounds.

"Are you lying?" she says roughly.

"No," I lie again. *Liar.* I hear an inside voice whisper. *Liar, liar, liar.* I feel sleazy. I feel dark. How do people lie regularly and come to terms with themselves? When it comes to Faye, I fluctuate between good and bad, danger and safety. I mean well, but take necessary actions . . .

I've got a present for you. Something you'll never forget.

"She's not my girlfriend," I say again. "You. You're my girlfriend."

Three days later, Meg calls in a rage. "Do you know what your favorite ex did?" she sputters.

I have no idea.

"She's a fuck. A fuck. A fuck, fuck, fuck," Meg hisses into the phone. "Playing me like I'm a fool. She agrees to the party, hell, she even meets me for lunch. Everything's arranged and then, I call her to confirm the details and she simply laughs and tells me to fuck off. 'Fuck off,' she says and hangs up on me. What was she doing? Just playing with me for the fun of it. I hate her. I hate her."

Faye can be rough, that's for sure. A player, yes. A fuck, yes. I knew that a long time ago.

"Did you speak to her? Have you two decided to have a party without me?" Fury lines her voice.

I close my eyes. "I suppose this means your party is canceled?" I say dreamily.

After all, Faye called last night. She's taking me to The Ritz for a birthday dinner.

"Three's a crowd," she said.

And I agreed.

Charm

"You and your so-called charm. Watch this!" Elaine picked up the voodoo doll she'd bought on a trip to New Orleans and twisted a needle into it. "Say *adios* to the ol' charisma." She waggled the doll in my face. "Those days are over."

The image of that doll — face blank, needle sunk in the chest — suddenly disappeared. I stood in the parking lot of the bar. How could Elaine even pretend to believe in that hocus-pocus crap?

I shoved my keys into my pocket and headed toward the entrance.

The bar was crowded, wild with women. Sifting through the haze of perfume and smoke, I headed toward the bartender. Each woman I passed made eye contact, smiled seductively, tilted her head as if to say, *yes*. And what wasn't to like? I had charm. I had charisma.

I felt heady. Intoxicated. Things were going to be fine . . . better than fine. So Elaine left me. So she said she'd had enough. So she promised I'd regret what I'd done. Voodoo doll be damned — I was on my way.

Sure, I felt bad — poor Elaine . . . hanging on to make-believe revenge. It was hard to blame her. After all, I did have that affair . . . But life goes on. The sooner she realized that, the better.

"Marta?"

At the bar and dressed to kill, Clarice waved me over. And why not? I was single. I was free. I had that certain something.

"Clarice. How've you been?" I signaled the bartender.

"Well . . . look who's finally out on the town." Clarice smiled seductively. Unbuttoned just enough to expose a hint of her white lacy bra, her silk green blouse was lush. A wide, leopard belt emphasized the curve from her waist to her round hips.

"Rumor had it that Elaine had you under lock and key . . . that is, up until the —"

"Life goes on," I interrupted. After all, there was no need to rehash the unsavory details of the affair.

"Things haven't been the same since you've been out of commission."

"Hey, Marta, welcome back." The bartender pushed a napkin in front of me. "Elaine finally let you have a night out?"

"We broke up."

"Whoa, sorry, I didn't know." She slid an ashtray across the bar. "You okay?"

"Sure, I'm okay. What's not to be okay about. I still got the old charm, don't I?" I gave her a smooth wink.

"Sure you do." A fast nod. "What can I get you?"

"Get her a night with me." Clarice laughed and touched my arm. Her perfume smelled like gardenias. A thin line of blue accentuated her dark eyes. Her lips were creamed in pale pink.

What wasn't to like about being single? I was compelling. No problems — not for me. I was footloose and fancy free. First night out on the town and already women were asking for a night with me.

I could imagine Elaine, sitting in that apartment, voodoo doll in hand. Perhaps she'd put the needle in the wrong place and accidentally made me more irresistible than I already was?

"Shot of tequila." I turned to Clarice. "And get her a night with me."

Another wink. A laugh. One drink. Two. Clarice and I — celebrating my newfound freedom. Celebrating my attractiveness.

"I just stopped seeing someone, too," Clarice offered out of the blue.

"Oh really?" I said, thinking, *Who cares?* I twisted the lime rind and dropped it into my empty glass. All that mattered was now, all that mattered was whether Clarice was interested in a toss with me.

"She follows me all the time."

Clarice's fingernails were painted the same shade as her seashell-tinted lips. I could imagine the feel of those nails digging into my back.

"Oh yeah? What's she trying to accomplish with that?" I did a quick scan of the room.

Clarice shrugged. "I guess she thinks she's intimidating."

"Doesn't intimidate me." Sounding tough, sounding cool, I squeezed Clarice's hand. All I could think of was getting us both out of the bar and tumbling into a big, soft bed.

"I've got a new car," Clarice murmured. "Want to go for a ride?"

Bingo! I was on my way.

Women wanted me, approached me, made the moves.

Looked to me like Elaine had herself a voodoo doll gone bad.

I dropped a twenty on the bar.

"Isn't this great?" Clarice was at the wheel of her new Mustang. A nice car. A hot woman. Everything was going my way.

"Oh shit! Shit! Shit!" Clarice adjusted the rearview mirror. "This is all I need."

"What? What?" I peered out the back window. A cop car, lights flashing a loud yellow, was closing in. But Clarice didn't slow down.

"God . . . now what?" she sputtered.

As if there was a choice as to what she should do! What the hell was she talking about? "What do you mean, *now what?* Pull over."

"I don't know —"

"Pull over, Clarice. Shit!"

"If I pull over, you got to do me a favor." We were still flying down the freeway.

"*If* you pull over, Clarice? Shit, this isn't a TV drama! You've got to stop. C'mon. Pull over!" I quick-glanced back at the cop. "C'mon! *Now!*"

"Okay! Okay!" she snapped. "But you've got to stall the cop for a minute . . . I know you can do it . . . use that charm of yours. I've got stuff in the glove compartment that I can't get caught with."

"Oh, God, Clarice, *what* stuff?"

"Just do it. Hurry."

She stopped the car along the side of the road. The cruiser pulled behind us. I popped the door open and climbed out. I had a few outstanding tickets myself. *Shit.*

I stepped in front of the cop. "Hello, Officer." A woman cop. Was that in our favor? "Guess we were going a little too fast. New car and all."

Suddenly, Clarice revved the engine and screeched onto the freeway. The red taillights disappeared into the black.

"What the hell? Hey! Clarice! Clarice!" What was she doing, leaving the scene like that? It was suspicious. Goddamned suspicious. "Officer, I don't know why she —"

Yet the cop didn't budge. She just stood there staring after Clarice's car. A peculiar expression soured her face.

Was the cop a dyke? Is that why she wasn't chasing after Clarice? She sure looked like one. Short-cropped hair. Rugged manner. Tough-ass stance. Maybe she's realized that I'm a dyke, too? Maybe she's offering us the benefit of the doubt?

Two butches on the side of a highway — a sort of unsaid common denominator underlined the situation. She'd let Clarice go . . . she was giving us a break.

A common denominator.

"You want to tell me what's going on." She turned from the empty dark where Clarice's car had been seconds ago and looked me right in the eyes.

One dyke to another on the side of a road. Things were going to be okay.

"I don't really know what to say . . ." I shrugged. "She offered to take me for a spin in her new car. You pulled us over and then she took off. I don't know why." I gave her one of my famous smiles. No sense keeping the old charm under wraps.

"Why'd you get out when she pulled over?" She put her hands on her hips.

"Because she asked me to?" I laughed but the cop didn't seem to see the humor.

"I'll need to see some ID, miss."

Miss? Oh God, *that* was a bad sign. A butch doesn't call another butch *miss*. Had I made a mistake? Shit — she *wasn't* a dyke? Maybe she hadn't raced after Clarice because she was concentrating on me? Shit . . . How many outstanding tickets *did* I have?

"Look, I haven't done anything. I'm a victim here, too." Stalling for time, I slowly pulled out my wallet.

"You calling me a victim?" The cop shot me a hard look.

"No, I'm just saying that I'm —"

"An accessory — that's what you are." She scanned my driver's license. "Hanging around the wrong people."

"I guess I made a mistake," I said apologetically. What the hell did she want from me?

"One hundred sixty pounds?"

I quickly glanced at her. "Yeah, I work out. It's the muscle."

She stepped back as though appraising me. "Is *that* right."

I suppressed a laugh. Double bingo! She was checking me out! Flirting! I'd been right all along — I was irresistible.

I was fifteen when I first realized the power of charm. Bev Gerhard and I used to hang out together — spending a lot of time down by Miller's store, acting cool. No matter what we were up to, Bev always managed to get us into trouble. In fact, my mom had given me a final warning . . . if Bev and I got into one more jam . . . no more Bev.

So Bev decided she wanted to steal a pack of cigarettes, and personally, although I had to agree that it did sound damn cool, I didn't think it was a great idea, what with Mrs. Miller being neighbors with the Gerhards.

But try to tell Bev no. Impossible. She took the cigarettes, and that was that. Until three days later when I was out for a walk and Mrs. Gerhard called to me from her front porch.

She said she'd found out about the cigarettes and that the whole thing put her in a very uncomfortable position. She opened the front door and I followed her in.

"Where's Bev?" I asked, glancing around the

living room. The place seemed extraordinarily quiet.

"She's off visiting her dad."

Mrs. Gerhard sat across from me in a wooden rocker. She was wearing a dark skirt with a pale cream blouse. She had probably just gotten home from her job at the bank. Sitting across from her like that, I could imagine her at work. In some stuffy bank president's office — maybe asking for a raise. Maybe asking for a bonus. She had that kind of smile . . . a smile that was asking for something extra special.

Mrs. Gerhard shifted in her chair. Her legs were slightly parted, making it impossible not to notice the lacy-pink panties she wore.

"I'd hate to call your mother, yet stealing *is* a serious crime." She tilted her head forward. Her raven hair curtained one blue eye.

I'd never taken a close look at Mrs. Gerhard before . . . after all, she *was* Bev's mom. But now that I had a chance, seeing her across from me, crossing and uncrossing those curvy legs, flashing that pink lace again and again, I had to admit she was very attractive.

"Look, Mrs. Gerhard . . ." I tried to sound casual. If my mom found out I had anything to do with stealing I'd be in major trouble. "I'm really just a victim here. I *told* Bev not to do it."

"Call me Lilith," Mrs. Gerhard said softly.

She pushed off her high heels. I could see all

the way up her skirt — how could I *not* notice? It was hard to focus on anything but that the delicious pink panty material and what lush flesh lay behind it.

"You know," Mrs. Gerhard said as she slowly swept the hair from her brow. "You seem *so* mature for your age."

Trying to pay attention, trying to pull my focus from that patch of pink lace, I nodded.

"You've got a certain something, a charm . . ." Mrs. Gerhard stood up, walked over to me, sat beside me on the couch. "Yes. Charm." She put her hand on my leg.

It was then that I understood that as far as the cigarettes were concerned, I was in the clear.

Yes . . . charm.

The cop reminded me of Lilith Gerhard in a sideways sort of way. She had that same look on her face that Mrs. Gerhard had when she'd crossed the room and put her hand on my thigh.

"I'm going to let you go this time." The cop handed me my driver's license. A heated desire streamed from her eyes.

I shoved the license into my pocket. Who needed Clarice when I had an opportunity like this? I had a certain something, a *je ne c'est pas*. Whether walking through a bar, sitting with

Clarice, talking with a cop ... let's face it ... I was drenched with it.

"I *really* should take you in, what with the suspicious nature of your story and all ..." Silence. "But I'm going to do you a favor and let you go." She didn't move.

"Well, thanks. Thanks a lot." I gave her my most charming smile.

The cop nodded. She liked me. It was written all over her face. "Perhaps I could do a favor in return?" I said smoothly.

"Perhaps you could." She smiled. "How about now? Right here."

I smiled. If there's one thing I believed in, it was respecting the law. I gestured toward the trees. "Want to take a little walk?"

She nodded and we headed for the woods.

"It's gotta be fast," she muttered.

"Fast as you want."

She grabbed my hand. She was leading the way ... looked like she was going to be in charge. Fine with me. A single woman, my life unfolding before me — tonight, I was the bottom. Tomorrow, with some other woman, I'd be on top. Whatever I wanted was mine.

I'd let her do whatever she pleased. We'd get behind a tree. Maybe she'd whisper in my ear. *What do you want? Huh? Huh, baby?* But she'd know what she'd *want* to do. Those authority types were all the same.

Maybe she'd handcuff me? Yeah, that would be good. She'd handcuff my arms around a tree. My face flush against the bark. I'd barely be able to move. How vulnerable! How helpless I'd be!

She'd undo my pants and pull them to my knees. She'd pull that nightstick from her belt. *I'm going to fuck you with this. Fuck you. Fuck you. Fuck you with this.* She'd inch the nightstick up my thigh — *we got to be fast* — and slip it against my damp, slick sex.

The bark is rough against my face. Maybe my shirt's open? Yeah, my shirt's ripped open and my breasts scrape the bark. My nipples are tight. My pussy is soaked.

I'd spread my legs as far as I could . . . and she'd jimmy the stick into my slit. Slow and easy. Nice and sweet — until I couldn't stand it anymore.

"C'mon," I'd cry.

"Sure, baby." She'd press the nightstick in further.

I clamp down hard. Tight — arch my ass higher.

She slides the stick in and out.

"Yes, oh yes. I like to be fucked. I need to be fucked."

"And I need to fuck you," she says low and harsh. The stick — in then out, in then out.

She'd see that I like it. She'd see how crazy I was for it. She'd pluck the nightstick out and

52

make me wait until finally, she'd squeeze it into my ass.

I'd let out a groan — but I'd like it. I'd cry out, but I'd need it. I'd squirm. I'd wiggle. But I'd like it, like it like it.

She'd twist it, turn it, screw it in and out of my secret crevice . . .

"How about right here?" Her voice pulled me out of my fantasy. We were at the edge of the woods.

"Sure, yeah, this is great." I was ready.

She pulled a pair of black handcuffs from her shirt pocket.

"Gotta be fast," she said again.

No problem. Fast was good.

She clamped one cuff around my wrist.

It's my charm that does it every time. One minute I was walking out of Elaine's house — with the not-so-discreet affair thrown in my face. But what, I'd asked Elaine, could I have done? When a woman has my kind of charm, it's hard to stay out of trouble.

The cop snapped the other handcuff to a low branch and pulled down my pants. Oh, this was going to be good. Good. Good. Good.

"About that favor." Her voice was suddenly gruff.

"Huh?"

"You know, the favor . . . you said you'd return the favor."

"Yeah, yeah." Anything she wanted. I was game.

"Stay the fuck away from Clarice." The cop briskly turned and headed for the cop car.

"What?" It felt like the breath had been knocked out of me.

The cop kept walking.

"Hey, wait a minute. Hey!"

The cop didn't look back. She just kept on walking until she reached her car, climbed in and pulled off.

One hand locked to a tree branch, I stared into the dark. What the hell! What the hell!

Someone would come by — *they had to.* Clarice. Of course, Clarice would come back. Hell, she was probably across the road, waiting. After all, women always come back to me . . . I've got that kind of appeal, I've got that kind of charm . . .

And somewhere across town, outside a darkened bedroom window, a voodoo doll hangs from the branch of a tree.

A Midsummer Night's Fantasy

"What a waste!" Laurel muttered as she grabbed her knapsack from the small boat and waded ashore. The best day of the summer — shit, the best day of the goddamn year and she was stuck with a Shakespeare Lit assignment that guaranteed a full day's commitment. Everyone else she knew was headed for the Women's Arts Festival.

Laurel followed the worn path up the side of the hill toward the forest. High in its midday ascent, the unveiled sun radiated. When she had rowed across the lake, the cool water had diminished the intensity of the heat but now, completely vulnerable, Laurel was well aware of the persistent sun. The shady shelter of the trees loomed ahead and Laurel quickened her pace.

Head down, counting hurried steps, Laurel was caught off guard when she slammed into another hiker.

"Oh —" Flustered, thrown off-balance, Laurel stumbled.

"Oh no, I wasn't watching where I was —" A strong, dark arm reached for Laurel and steadied her. "You okay?"

"Yes, I —" Laurel stopped mid-sentence. The woman — whose firm, warm hand still held Laurel's arm, whose obsidian eyes glimmered with mystery, whose sultry scent was like an aura — stood before her. Laurel debated a mock swoon — tumble to the ground, have this woman swoop her into a powerful embrace? Laurel could only imagine the strength, the passion those sculptured arms could generate.

"I'm so sorry. I wasn't watching where I was going . . ." The woman hesitated as though something more would be said, as though, perhaps, something more was indeed *being* said, yet she was silent.

"No, I was daydreaming," Laurel offered. Once

again, she surreptitiously appraised the stranger's magnificent build and sincerely wished she'd been knocked to the ground.

Almost as if an afterthought, the woman released Laurel's arm. "Well, it was nice running into you." She flashed an amused smile, then continued past Laurel.

Laurel stood motionless, unable to do anything but watch the woman who had a walk that could bring marching bands to a abrupt halt. An overpowering urge to call out, "No, wait, come back!" swept through her. And what, Laurel argued with herself, ask this stranger to hold me? Kiss me? Make love to me? As if such a thing were possible! As if the woman would even be interested . . .

"Lord what fools these mortals be," Laurel mumbled, staring across the empty landscape. Her woman had disappeared somewhere down the hill. With a heavy sigh, Laurel kicked a rock down the path and begrudgingly headed toward Shakespeare and the waiting forest.

There was a place, not too deep in woods, that Laurel called her own. One day last spring, while searching for blackberries, she had discovered her paradise. Wandering down an overgrown path thickly walled with bushes, Laurel had come across a small area, virtually unspoiled by the usual barrage of island hikers. Here she came to soothe her wounds, dream her dreams or, as today, read — I don't want to, rather be at the women's festival — Shakespeare.

She pushed her way through the thicket, not surrendering to the persistent branches that challenged her with sharp, fast scrapes. The reward — the large tree she'd lean against, the soft grass she'd sit upon, finally came into view.

From the knapsack, Laurel unfolded a thin quilt. She tossed a pen, a pad of paper and her copy of *A Midsummer Night's Dream* onto the spread and gratefully kicked her shoes aside. Shakespeare, here I come, she thought and leaned back against the tall oak.

The forest was tranquil, so tranquil that a weary hiker could fall asleep — if the trek had been long, if the sun had been hot, if the words from the play she read soothed like a lullaby. Laurel drifted in and out of Shakespeare's whimsical settings until she slipped, unaware, into a dream . . .

. . . And the air was hot. In a sheer floral dress, she danced in circles across the open clearing. Surrounding trees enclosed the field like tall green guards, and Laurel did fairy-like pirouettes in the sun.

A seductive shadow weaving between the trees seemed to follow her from the periphery. Laurel was uncertain, yet she sensed the dark eyes, those obsidian eyes, watching from the forest. Around and around, like a spiraling snowflake, Laurel twirled to please her hidden audience.

From the forest, the shadowy figure stepped into the sun. The heat sharpened, heightened, driving Laurel's dance toward a slow, dizzy halt. With a steady pace, the mysterious spectator came to the center of the clearing, came to the lacy ballerina and with one strong hand, completely stopped the faltering spin.

At first the trees, the sky, the entire field still whirled, but even though temporarily disoriented, Laurel knew all too well who had grabbed her from behind. She recognized the strength, the power, the passion of the simple gesture — a firm, warm hand on her slender arm. The woman from the path had followed her, had come for her.

"You," Laurel said softly. Pleasantly light-headed, she turned to face the woman of her dreams. Instead, a bewildering creature stood before her.

The trim, muscular body, the onyx eyes were definitely those of the woman. But the face — the entire head! — was that of a beautiful bronco.

"I have wanted you from that moment on the path." The horse spoke in a low, clear tone.

Speechless, Laurel stared into the horse's eyes and felt the distinct sensation of free-falling. Into the cool blackness, into the inky depths of those eyes, Laurel wanted to dive. The sun beat against her back. Too hot. Too, too hot. She felt suddenly weak, as if her legs would no longer support her, as if the grass-covered ground would soon give way.

In a swift motion, the horse-woman lifted Laurel, carried her across the field to a large, flat rock. The surface was rough and her sheer dress snagged slightly as the horse-woman lay her on the stone altar.

"Are your thighs as creamy as the dress you wear?" the horse-woman asked as she slowly raised the sheer fabric higher on Laurel's legs.

Laurel moaned as her dress was pulled up to her waist. She glanced into the horse-woman's eyes, then to her sturdy shoulders and finally to her bulging biceps, one arm decorated with a tattooed tangle of black roses.

The horse-woman separated Laurel's legs and stepped between them. She tore open the top of Laurel's dress to reveal thick, erect nipples.

Laurel arched her back. Do you like what you see, she thought as she strained her tits high. Do you?

"Your nipples," the horse-woman said as she plucked each one, then both together, "are incredible." She squeezed hard. Hard enough to cause Laurel to yelp in pleasurable pain.

With one fast snap, Laurel's silk panties were ripped aside. Her legs were spread further. Her pussy was completely exposed and the sun — the delicious, pounding hot sun — poured liquid heat directly onto her slippery, pink sex.

Laurel moaned.

"Do you want to go for a ride, my pretty Princess?" the horse-woman murmured between short, quick breaths. Not waiting for an answer, she stretched the fleshy lips wide and sunk a finger into the pearl sap. "How far? Huh, pretty Princess? How far and how fast do you want to go?"

Two fingers? Three fingers? Laurel was unsure. They were big, they were rough, they filled her like nothing ever had before. Laurel raised her hips, attempting to push those fingers farther, deeper. But the horse-woman continued her journey at an excruciatingly slow, deliberate pace.

Four fingers? Five? Eyes closed, teeth clenched, Laurel tried to relax the involuntary tight clamping of her vaginal muscles. Now thicker, now larger, now wider, the hand pushed in. Laurel's pussy felt packed, as if that hand were more than a hand. As if that hand were much, much more.

The horse-woman, her hand buried up to her wrist, let out a long cry and then broke into a fast plunge.

Laurel's cry rivaled the horse-woman's. She felt as if she were racing bareback. She was galloping, thundering across a wide-open plain on an unbroken stallion. It felt like fingers, then a fist and finally a solid, thick hoof inside her. Didn't matter. It was good, it was hard and it took her far, farther than she could imagine. Farther than she had ever been.

"Ride me good. Ride me good!"

She slammed down on the hoof. It rammed high into her, harder and harder until Laurel disappeared in a dust storm of violent pleasure . . . .

Laurel slammed out of her dream. Her back, pressed hard against the rough tree bark, felt scraped and raw. She felt dizzy, slightly disoriented, but completely satiated. Her book, still opened on her lap, revealed pages that were crinkled and torn.

What time it was, Laurel didn't know, but the air was cooler and the sun no longer occupied its midday throne.

Lazily, Laurel gathered her belongings. She'd go home. She'd finish her reading tonight, she thought, no longer in the mood to sit idly in the woods. She headed back to the main path, down the hill toward her small canoe. Every muscle ached. It was there, not too far from where Laurel had come ashore, that she saw the woman, apparently asleep on a large blue blanket.

Laurel approached slowly. The woman, who had removed her shirt and was sunning in a bathing suit, didn't stir. Perhaps thirty, maybe forty steps in that direction would lead her to where the woman lay. One hundred steps or so to the right was the boat.

Five steps toward the boat. Five more. Laurel stopped and took one more look at the sun-soaked sleeper. It was then that she saw the tangled black tattoo on the woman's arm.

Laurel took another step. Then another . . .

Ten Years Ago

A last-minute invitation has brought me back to this beach house. Jeanie called for a reunion of the old gang and all six of us came. I haven't been here since the days spent with Margo. A move to the East Coast took me far from Dillon Beach, the West Coast, and the memories of her.

Ten years ago I sat on this very beach and shielded my eyes to get a better view of the woman who walked down by the water's edge. The sun surrounded her in a sparkling glow. A shimmering silhouette, she moved like a butterfly fluttering between the ocean and me.

I sit here this early evening and watch the oncoming waves push to shore. The ocean's hypnotic song is the only sound. *Remember?* The relentless sea seems to whisper. *Remember? Remember?*

The red-orange sun melts into dusk like heated sherbet. I stare out to the horizon. Wasn't it only a moment ago that the sky was blue, the sun was high? Wasn't it just a turn-of-the-head ago that I had shielded my eyes to watch her move like a dancer across this beach?

In a tidal wave, thoughts of her rush toward me. Overwhelming. Unstoppable. This very moment is what I have been avoiding all these years. The rest of the gang is back at the house preparing dinner. A reckless whim has led me from the house, across the deck, down the steps and to the sea. I sit in the place I had sat ten years before — when I had first seen Margo, called to her, climbed out of my chair to find out more . . .

"Hey!" I called, uncertain why. Perhaps it was the way the straw hat was pulled low over her eyes or how her semi-transparent skirt flowed around her like a spring flower in bloom. Something about her — a softness? a mysteriousness? — compelled me to keep her from simply passing by.

She stopped and turned. "This a private beach?"

Without thought, I climbed out of the chair and headed toward her. And yes, this was a private beach, and yes, I had permission to be here and she didn't — yet a sense of surrender overcame me as I approached her. The heated sand beneath my bare feet shifted from harsh dryness to cool and damp. The glaring sun yielded to a refreshing ocean breeze. And I, a woman normally tough and certain of myself in any situation, suddenly felt soft and buttery.

"Yeah, it's private. But lucky for you, I've got connections with the owners." I noted the sprinkling of freckles across her face. Tied back in a low pony tail, her long, ebony hair hung halfway down her back. Her dark brown eyes were swirled cinnamon and chocolate. I regarded the tint of her plush lips. Were they not as lush as the succulent raspberries Jeanie had served for brunch only hours before?

"A woman with connections, huh? Lucky for me," she teased. She crossed her arms and swayed coquetishly back and forth.

Goddamn, was she flirting with me? I ran my hand through my close-cropped hair and considered my options. In the bars, I always knew what was what with the women, but on a beach — in the middle of nowhere and out of my element — God only knew who was a dyke and who wasn't . . .

The vision of Margo in her summer skirt flickers then dissipates. The sun has sunk into the inky ocean and I am left empty-handed on a lonely beach. The sudden chill attempts to persuade me to return to the beach house and the warmth of old friends. I glance to the sea.
Remember? Remember?
At dusk, shadows along the water's edge become difficult to distinguish. The waves rise like reminisced love then crash into the foam-embroidered sand.
Remember? Remember?
Is that something riding the waves far on the horizon? I squint. I stand. I bury my hands in my jacket pockets and take several steps toward the water.
Remember? Remember?
The ocean laps the sand in quick, intent strokes. The brisk air tells me to turn back, but a figure cruises the rough water toward the shore and I am immobilized. A mirage — certainly a mirage — moves across the dark water. As if there was some way she could ride from the edge of the

world toward me, I sense Margo on the crest of that wave racing from the past to the present.

Margo? I am uncertain if I have actually called out for her or if the ocean is crying out to me. Somehow I have moved. The water sloshes against my boots. I don't care.

Margo? The full moon climbs the sky and spills a pearly glaze across the sea. A ballet dancer pirouettes on a moonlit wave. Ten long years ago, she came to me.

If only I could take her in my arms this very moment and show her how I've learned to love . . .

We had sat close to the ocean. She curved spirals in the damp sand with one polished fingernail. Her skirt was bunched and her tanned thighs were revealed. All I could think of was raising that skirt and tracing spirals along her smooth, dark skin with my tongue. The straw hat was still low on her brow. Her top was lacy white. A strand of creamy pearls formed a perfect circle of tiny moons. I knew that from that second on, whenever I'd see a full-orbed moon, I would think of her jeweled neck.

"The Queen of Swords." She pulled a tarot card from her skirt pocket, glanced at the image of an icy woman seated on a throne and then peered at me. "I'm destined to meet her. She's supposed to ask something of me that changes my life." She gathered three tiny rocks from the sand and threw them toward the water. "Are you familiar with the cards? My husband thinks I'm weird because I put so much meaning into these sort of things."

The words *my husband* flitted around us like black gulls. I felt wreathed in a thin, dark breeze. Hadn't she been flirting? Her gauze skirt had slipped even higher on her thighs. Her husband. Her husband.

"Doesn't sound weird to me," I offered. I tossed my own pebble. I had a question or two for her that could change her life, all right. Layna used to read the cards. Was the Queen of Swords a dyke? "Queen of Swords, huh?" I glanced at the card.

"She's a strong woman who goes after what she wants," Margo said, almost wistfully. "The sword of spirit penetrates."

"So do I," I said offhandedly. I stared straight into the horizon and thought about my words. *So do I.* The implications weren't clear. So do I go after what I want or so do I penetrate? I withheld an urge to laugh. "I mean, go after what I want." My hand rested in the cool sand, only millimeters away from her thigh, only millimeters away from her warm skin. I allowed my finger the luxury of inching onto her floral skirt.

Was it possible that she didn't know I was a dyke? Was it feasible that she was oblivious to what everyone, all my life, had pointed out, snickered at and finally tried to deny? My short hair was slicked back — and I looked like a dyke. A pack of cigarettes was rolled into the sleeve of my T-shirt — and I looked like a dyke. Jangling from the belt loop of my jeans was a set of keys — and I looked like a dyke. Scuffed and well-worn, my work boots lay untied in the sand — and looked like they'd been worn by a dyke. And just in case this wasn't enough, the tattoo on my forearm did little to dissuade from the rest of the lesbian package. Perhaps she knew exactly what she was dealing with ... and why.

Married, femmed-up and sitting quite close, Margo had engaged me in a conversation about the spirit of penetration. It was difficult not to speculate exactly what kind of cards she was *really* looking to play.

She whispered something under her breath. I turned to catch her words and saw a lone tear working its way down her cheek.

"Are you okay?" I said softly. My hand had somehow found its way to that silkiness of her skirt.

Margo shrugged and bowed her head. Like nature's symphony of rhythmical waves or her orchestration of polychrome sunsets, a natural movement began between us. Gently, respectfully, I encircled Margo in my arms and held her while she cried . . .

My boots are soaked. My feet drenched. Daylight has folded into itself leaving me engulfed by the black satin night. I stare at the moon and think of her necklace. Those iridescent pearls had graced her regal neck like a snowy halo.

On this very beach she had cried — perhaps only a few yards? feet? inches? from where I now stood. The high tide rushes in, nips at my ankles then flows back to mother sea. Embedded in the saturated sand, a curved rock protrudes like a stubborn tortoise. A swift kick sends it somewhere down the beach.

Margo? Margo?

My jacket is thin and does little to protect me from the cold air. Turning back is no longer an option. Not any more. Not when Margo is so close — riding the waves from past to present. So close — soaring from a wave crest like a entrancing sea nymph.

Do I dare walk farther down the beach? Climb the dunes? Lie in the place where, that star-draped night, we lay ten years ago . . . ?

* * * * *

It was on her last night at Dillon Beach that we climbed the dunes. All week, the sunset had been our ally. At dusk we'd meet, stroll down the beach, then head home. Her last night, and I was desperate not to let it end without telling her how I felt, without kissing her or taking her in my arms.

Each night, I'd thought only of her. Fantasies of what I'd do the next time we met filled the long late hours before sleep — how I'd kiss her with the same determination as the swollen tide. With the same unchecked liberties taken by the moon, I'd caress her, bathe her in the pleasures of liquid silver and gold.

We reached the dunes. She turned, ready to head back, ready to let our last night simply disappear like a sand castle beneath the rushing sea. I peered at the night sky. I would memorize every star before I let her go.

Did the ripe moon have a slow leak? At the week's onset, it had been extravagant in its golden promises. This night, the full yellow circle seemed slightly eaten away. No longer complete. No longer perfect.

There was no reason to speak. After all, the agitated ocean would sweep away any words — scatter them like driftwood. It was the thoughts that mattered, the intentions. Her last night and chances were meant to be taken. Her last night and choices had to be made. Without a word, I took her hand and led her up the sandy hill.

Her silence revealed nothing, yet everything. Between the dunes — sheltered from the breeze, safeguarded from the boundaries of who we were down on that beach, down on the cold sand that led from her beach house to here — we trekked.

It was chilly, I didn't care. I unzipped my jacket and laid it in a hollowed alcove between two dunes. We sat down and the cold air could no longer test us. We sat down and the string of lit beach houses, lined like beacons in the night, could no longer call to us. We sat down and suddenly, there was nothing to distract us. It was simply she and I.

"Margo?" I whispered her name. The single word coiled around me in a long, heated breeze. *Margo, can I kiss you? Margo, can I touch you? Margo, can I be your lover, just tonight, just once, before he takes you back to Montana?*

She turned toward me. The moon glittered a diamond light in her eyes. Her swept-back hair was silky midnight. Wasn't there something I had wanted to ask her? It was her lips, the color of dark wine, that had suddenly distracted me, that had suddenly forced me to forget everything but the feel of ruby satin.

Her mouth. Her mouth was ambrosia — full, thick. All I could think of was the softness of rose petals, the sweetness of fresh berries, the creamy warmth of a kiss. Each night I had walked the beach with her, listening to her joys and sorrows.

I never shared mine. I longed to hold her — could I tell her that? I wanted to take her in my arms and give her the things she wanted — could I tell her that? Instead, I kept my dreams hidden in the pocket of my flannel shirt.

"Margo?"

Silence. She had folded her hands in her lap. Her skirt flowed over her crossed legs to laced boots.

In that moment, I could have dived into the velvet of her succulent lips. I could have spent a thousand years lost in the luxury of one solitary kiss. Was I not butch? Was I not the Queen of Swords — quick and confident in all she does? If I traced my finger along her check, if I brushed the wisp of fallen hair from her brow, if I kissed her lightly on her neck, would she race down the dunes in a flurry of disappointment?

I want to kiss you. My unspoken words seemed louder than my pounding heart. I was certain she heard my thought. But before I could ask, before I could make my desire known, Margo leaned close and kissed me lightly on the cheek. She started to pull back but my hand, seemingly acting on its own, pushed into her ebony hair and with the gentlest of pressure, stopped her retreat.

"Margo, no, please don't pull away." I drew her to me. My anxious lips caressed her cool cheek. The scent of her perfume carried me to a field of midsummer flowers. She and I, hand in hand, danced in a hurricane of multi-colored petals. She and I lay in a bed of long, gentle grass.

I was hungry for more of her, starving for more. Down her cheek, to her neck. The pearls were smooth against my lips. I kissed one, then another, finally kissing my way around the ivory circle of moons.

"Margo. Margo. Margo." My words were smothered in her neck. Suddenly impatient, I worked my way to her chin, to her cheek and then to the oblivion of her moist lips.

One kiss and I was free-falling. One kiss and I was submerged in undulating waves of desire. My fingers slid under her skirt — and I kept kissing her. Her skin was soft beneath my fingers — and I kept kissing her.

She lay back. I moved on top of her. Stirred. On fire. I just lay there. Her breasts were full beneath my chest — was I too heavy? I knew how unhappy she was. How much weight she could actually bear. How ravenous she was for something more.

A savage power surged through me. A scorching need to take her, to show her, to bring her to the place she longed to go. The Queen of Swords penetrates, does she not? Does she not?

I raised her sweater. I pushed her blouse out of my way. Hundreds of fast kisses spilled from my mouth onto her curved belly. I nipped. I bit. If

I could have devoured her, sucked her completely into me, I would have.

Her bra was pink lace. I liked that. I pulled the cup down and her areola immediately wrinkled. How cool the air was! How crisp!

Margo moaned. She writhed. I squeezed her thick nipple between my fingers, twisted it, pinched it and Margo began to grind her hips. She grabbed at my hair, pressed her mouth against my neck.

I lowered the bra cup from her other breast. That nipple lifted up in grateful anticipation. In a second, my mouth covered it, suckled it, rolled it. Margo. Margo. Margo. The Queen of Swords penetrates.

Under her skirt, my hand raced up her thigh to the soaked panty crotch. Her pussy lips bulged under the lacy material. With one finger, I tugged her panties aside.

The hair was like fine corn-silk. Oh yes. Oh yes. Margo. Margo. Margo. Into the swollen sex-flesh, I slid one finger. I slipped my finger between the buttery folds until I found her tiny nugget.

Margo got crazy. She bucked beneath me. She pounded my back. She wrapped her legs around my hips and rocked like a wild woman. I knew women — it was penetration she wanted, penetration she craved.

I flicked her sex-bead with my finger ---
plucked it and nudged it again and again. Margo
was jerking. Crying. Pleading.

I had her. I had her good. My fingers swam
across her ribbed slit, to the raised portal. Back
to the gem-hard clit. I made circles, fast figure-
eights, slow loops across, around and over her
clitoris.

Margo. Margo. Margo.

I inched one fingertip into her. Tight, greasy,
wet. I buried another fingertip, then another. And
then, without regard, I slammed her. Without
reservation, I sunk into her, plunged into her,
pounded into her, again and again.

I bounced my hips against her while I rocked
her good. Up and down, I moved on her. I
burrowed three, then four fingers deep inside. She
was warm. She was slippery. Faster and faster, I
went. I worked. I gave her what she needed, what
I needed. I fucked her, I had her. I was driving
her, pumping her. My clit felt rock-hard. I was
ready to explode — moving on my woman, gliding,
sliding, flying on my woman. On a hard come,
riding my woman, I crashed into orgasm. She
arched her back. A trembling energy shot through
her as she came and I came. Sex cream sputtered
all over my hand. Margo. Margo. Margo. Her head
tilted back and then to the side. A wave of
agonizing pleasure flowed over her face. She bit

her lip and shuddered. I cried her name into the night.

Margo. Margo. Margo.

And then all was quiet.

My hand was soaked with her sweat, her desire. She opened her eyes. The tension in her face had softened into a beautiful smile.

"Oh Anne." She touched my face, then ran her finger along my jaw to my neck. She began unbuttoning my shirt.

I shook my head and took her hand in mine. With her other hand, she tried again.

No.

No one touches me. I get my pleasures from pleasing my woman. On top of her, in her, behind her, that is my pleasure.

"Can't I touch you too? Can't I please you too?"

"Oh God, Margo. You already have." I wrapped her in my arms and for a brief moment, lying with Margo, I contemplated what it would be like to lie under a woman, to take off my clothes, to have her fingers push into me . . .

One moment I'm on the private beach below Jeanie's house, the next I'm standing at the foot of the dunes. I wonder how long I've been standing here, staring up at the mound of sand. If I climb the dune, will I find her, sitting in the alcove waiting for me?

The hammering ocean reverberates with memories. She cried when I pushed her hand away. She couldn't grasp why I was so adamant. *"Is it because I would disappoint you?"* she had asked. *"Is it because I've never touched a woman?"*

And how could I have explained what I hadn't understood myself? Walking back to the beach houses without talking, I felt like a failure. She felt worse. She kissed me and then disappeared into her future, alone and without me.

Layna read my cards that night. I remember the Queen of Swords was upside down. I remember wishing I could go to her place, grab her hand, let her take me into the dark and love me back.

I take a step up the dune.

Margo? Have I actually called her name out or is it just the restless sea? A tear flirts on my eyelash.

Margo?

Everyone is at the beach house cooking dinner. Friends for years, buddies for life. Was it nine years ago? eight? when things started to change? When someone — Layna? Jeanie? Carol? — started telling the truth about how empty she felt, how isolated she was ... hell, how lonely *we* all were.

I climb farther up the dune. The sea breeze whips around me. *Go home!*

Years passed, more conversations, more sharing, opening up, acceptance. Slowly, we began to like ourselves, to feel proud about who we were. And everywhere there were rainbow flags, marches, parades. Books were being written, magazines were telling our stories.

The gang started to change. We began to blossom into ourselves. Some of us grew our hair long. Some of us wore lipstick. We did what we wanted and dressed how we felt ...

Almost to the top of the dune.

We were touching and being touched. And if Margo were here tonight ...

Margo? Margo?

She could love me now. She could take me now.

I stand at the top of the dune and peer into the darkened alcove. A shadow? A memory? I shake my head to clear my vision. Is that Margo, sitting cross-legged in the alcove? She is smoking a cigarette. Her hair is shaved on the sides. She wears a leather jacket and motorcycle boots.

"Margo?"

A mirage? A vision? She grinds her cigarette into the sand.

"Anne?"

She stands. With a smile she removes her jacket and lays it in the sand — like I had done for her, so many years before.

Ten long years melt into a single minute. I slide down the sand to capture my dream.

Daddy's Girl

You said you wanted to be my daddy, for just one night. Like a sharp, quick stiletto the notion penetrated me and I thought, *I don't need no daddy. Not me. Not anymore.* I bit my tongue, said nothing.

"For one night, for one solitary night." Your voice was as smooth as a high-stake gambler holding a royal flush.

No way. Even so, a sudden thirst parched my

mouth and a hard-hitting hunger churned in the pit of my stomach.

"I could be your daddy for just tonight," you whispered. "It could be so good. I'd be so nice to my sweet, sweet girl."

In that moment, when you said those words, your eyes made promises, scorching promises. Wordless pacts can only be made when lovers like you and I connect. The heat between us fanned the gnawing from my belly to my heart. A sensation of starvation swept through me.

"Yes, okay," I said, looking toward the floor.

Your fingers lightly traced my chin. "You seem unsure." You already sounded like a daddy. My daddy.

I shrugged. "Maybe a little," I said in a voice that seemed far away.

You pulled a pink ribbon from your pocket and tied it in my hair.

"Or maybe," you said, tender as a spring bud, "I could just be the person who's always loved you, the one who has watched you grow and waited until you were old enough to love me too."

I nodded. Anything you've ever wanted, I'd give to you, and more. You know this.

"Is that what you want?" My words travel from the distance.

You tightened the bow, my hair in a ponytail, and I imagine? you imagine? *We* imagine bobby socks and saddle shoes. It's like that with us, fantasy flows like slow-moving waves and who we are transforms. Leaving time behind, you and I go anywhere we please. Our love is a safety net for trapeze leaps and I trust you and love you and follow your lead. Jumping across the abyss to meet you in the infinite unknown. You wait for me there. It's so good. I close my eyes and fly through the air to your outstretched hand and never fear missing — never fear the fall or sudden impact or that you won't be there. You will, always are and you tie my hair in a pony tail because you like it that way and it's wrong and it's right and I hardly care.

You take my hand and we cross the room to a different year. I remember you — you have always loved me, from the time I was too small to tie a shoe and there we are now. You are hesitant because love can be too right and too wrong, all at once.

You love me, don't you?

Yes. I hear your response strong and clear.

Of course you do, you always have. You've watched me grow from a little girl and you've tied my shoes and you've tied my hair and your hand touches my breast — swollen with youth — and I'm dizzy and weak and hungry for you.

And haven't you loved me for all this time?

Your hand slides from my breast to my thigh and I ache with a longing both ancient and new.

"Is this okay?" You ask and we both know it is, but it's not, but it is. I'm young and alive and you've known me since I was only this tall. I fly

85

through the air with the greatest of ease and your love is the place where I'm soaring, free.

I have no doubts, not with you. I don't look down, I look straight to you, to your outstretched hand. And you're coming toward me, reaching for me . . .

Your outstretched hand moves to my dampness, moves to my sex and I'm young and uncertain and love you more than life itself. I think maybe it's wrong, but it feels too right, and I'm old enough *now* to make this choice. And haven't you loved me all this time?

My hair is tied back with a pretty pink bow and I close my eyes and free-fall into your love, not fearing, not caring about the boundaries I've broken.

And your fingers sink into the place that is warm. I'm hungry for you, desperate for you and the gnawing has turned to an avalanche of desire. I spread my legs for you, I arch up for you.

And I fly through the air. The love that you have is my destined trapeze. Your fingers are strong. Your fingers go deep. Pleasure shoots through me as if I've been asleep — all these years. You've known me forever and loved me so long, together our joy sings an unending song.

No safety net compares to a woman like you. I know it. You know it. God, it's so true. The tie in my hair makes me young and alive. Your fingers push in, your hand grasps my thigh.

I'm yours tonight and tonight you are mine.

Tonight and tomorrow, and forever in time. You care for me, like only you can, and I leap to connect with your far-reaching hand.

And we dive in the air, tumble in the air, roll, thunder, collide in the air. Round and round, together we whirl — my daddy, my lover and her little girl.

Variations

I arrived at the restaurant ten minutes early. This was one date I didn't want to be late for. First time I'd ever answered the Personals, but after a messy breakup and no sex for a month, an ad titled *Imagination* from a woman who promised "a hot night of variation" was right up my alley.

I scanned the bar. On a stool, halfway to the back wall, sat a red-haired femme fatale. Like liquid licorice, her black silk dress flowed over her curvaceous body. She shifted slightly and a teasing flash of her black-stockinged thigh was provocatively revealed. Her panther eyes locked into mine. *Over here.*

I pointed at her —*Are you the one?* —and smiled.

She nodded, slowly slid off the stool and headed toward me. She had an I-want-to-be-fucked walk that made my knees weak. I swallowed hard and held my ground.

She stepped in close. "Are you my date?" Her voice was smooth and slippery and her predatory eyes zeroed in on me.

I thought back to her ad, laden with sexual promises, and then made my move. "Imagination, right?"

She grabbed my arm. I could feel her nails through my shirt sleeve. "Come to the restroom with me." She licked her pink lips. "I'll give you just what you need. Something new. Something different."

She dug her nails in deeper. Her perfume surrounded me in a thick haze. Her nipples stood like hard sentinels beneath her flimsy dress. Something new? In the restroom? This wasn't quite what I had had in mind —but variation *was* what the ad had promised, wasn't it?

She pulled me through the crowded Italian restaurant to the restroom. It was small with an old, velvet-covered chair crammed in the corner.

Two stalls lined the wall. Above the sink hung an antique, circular mirror.

"Brand new —" Her words were hurried and short as she pulled a black harness from her purse. "Like nothing you've ever experienced."

The big mystery was a dildo harness? Shit, every woman I knew already owned one. "Like nothing I've ever experienced, huh?" I said, not hiding my amusement. "I don't think so . . ." I shook my head in mock disappointment. "I've already got one."

"Not like *this*." Her voice deepened. "Let me show you. Please." Red-hot innuendo lined her words. "Please?"

With an ice-melting smile, she slipped a thick dildo into the harness, rolled a condom over it and moved in front of me. "It's a thigh harness, it slips on like this —" She strapped the dildo around my thigh. "What's nice," she continued in her maple syrup voice, "are the variations one can do." She pushed me into the chair, then raised her skirt. I glanced at the door. She had locked it, hadn't she?

She wore no panties. The lush dark hair that covered her pretty pussy barely concealed the pink, dangling inner lips. "When you're sitting, I can straddle you."

I took a deep breath as she lowered herself onto the thick dildo that was strapped to my leg. Her skirt was hiked high. Her pussy lips, beaded with tiny white drops, sliced apart as the dildo head teased. Time seemed to stretch into long, desperately slow moments. A thunderous pleasure throbbed in my pussy as I watched the dildo flirt with her strawberry-tinted flesh.

She took her sweet time — rotating her hips like a stripper, smearing her sopping pussy on the smooth head. I couldn't take it. I grabbed her waist. I wanted to jam into her. Fuck her like the little tease deserved. I rammed her down, pulled her up. Plunged her back down, lifted her back up. She groaned. She sighed. She got crazy — grabbing at my shirt, pulling at my hair. "Yeah, baby, c'mon, baby!"

Suddenly, the restroom door creaked open. My heart dropped and my face went beet-red. A breathtaking woman appraised us carefully then locked the door.

"So do you like the new thigh harness?" she said seductively. "What's nice —" She walked over to the woman on my leg and gave her a nice long kiss. "— are the variations one can do."

And with that, she pulled a dildo-laden harness from her purse. Within seconds, her skirt was up, the harness was strapped to my other leg and both women were riding me. They kissed. They opened each other's dresses and squeezed each other's hard, red nipples. My hands raced across their full breasts, dipped into their wet pussies.

A vibrator was handed to me — God, I loved women with imagination — and I pushed it against my pussy. Through my pants, the vibrator buzzed. I was reeling. I was rolling. I moved the vibrator from pussy to pussy. And they fucked my legs until we all blasted into hard-driving pleasure.

Next day, I purchased three thigh harnesses. One for myself — I figured I could strap it onto the seat of a stool and fly solo ... and two extras to appease my ever-expanding imagination.

After all, what's nice about thigh harnesses are the variations ...

Baseball

Sports enthusiast? Me? Well . . . I suppose so.
No, I don't play soccer. Baseball, volleyball,
basketball? No. So what *do* I play? I play rough. I
play hardball. I play with the best. Sport erotics,
that's my game.

Oh yeah, act like you don't know what I'm
talking about. Act like you go to those games to
watch a ball be smacked by a stick or tossed over
a net. Nothing like that kind of excitement? Yeah,
right.

I tell the truth about athletic events. A sport is a sport, wherever it's played. Doesn't make much difference to me. Whether on a field or in a gym — tie a bandanna around a woman's head, show off her thighs in a pair of shorts, tease me with her biceps in a short-sleeved shirt and that's what I call a good game.

Take baseball. Tough-faced, with a jock swagger that could knock me from the bleachers, the batter approaches the plate. Shoulders back, attitude seeping like thick honey, the woman means business. Damn. If she's got that much intensity on the field, imagine what she'd be like in bed.

I watch her tap the bat against her cleats. Her weight shifts from foot to foot and her hips rock slightly. Nice ass, great ass, she bends slightly and does a warm-up swing. She's serious, all right. It's written all over her face. I like a woman with a one-track mind; a woman who can focus on the subject at hand.

I visualize myself across from her with a pitcher's mitt. High heels, garter belt, a bright red baseball hat — sure, I know about uniforms. She looks me straight in the eye with fierce, butch concentration. I toss her a pouty, little smile. *You ready for a curve ball?*

Her eyes drop from mine and skim my tight, thin tank top. Strike one. I'm looking good, I'm looking fine.

Nervous, caught off-guard, she shoots me a

lucky-break smirk. I spread my legs slightly. My high heels pierce the dirt, the tank-top rides high on my midriff. Strike two.

Yeah, baby, oh baby. I'm hot now. A harsh edge replaces the batter's smirk. She doesn't like my sassy attitude? I don't care. Let her come to the pitcher's mound if she's got a problem. Let her come right up and show me what she wants, show me exactly how she'd like me to do it for her.

Last inning, last chance. The score is tied. A tense silence blankets the crowd. Women in the stands, women on the sidelines — they all have their eyes on me. Can I do it again? Can I bring her to her knees?

The sweet scent of desire spins from the batter and surrounds me in a sudden heat. Unbridled power spills from her strong arms, her thick hands, her muscular thighs. Our eyes lock. She's ready for it. She's hungry for it.

I caress the baseball against my smooth fingers and consider her firm breasts. An immediate compulsion to drop the ball, rush to home plate and press my desperate hands against her overwhelms me.

Breaking rules, playing dirty, she looks at me with fire in her eyes. It's clear she could take me. It's clear she could suck me dry. Light-headed, I hold the ball close to my face. I focus, zero in on the imaginary line between us. Sparks dart from her eyes, her mouth, her fingertips.

She has me. She has me good. I throw the ball. It slices the air and the crowd begins to roar. Let her run. Let her go wherever she wants. I drop the mitt, I head toward first base. If she slides, let her ram into me. I can take it hard. I can take it as hard as she can give it.

The ball soars across the field and she leaps, as though in slow motion, to first base, second, then third. Her thighs are tight with power, her arms slice through the hot, summer air.

C'mon. C'mon, C'mon.

An explosion of pleasure races through me. Her ass is taut. Her eyes, determined. Into home she slides. I want her more than anything. I'd do anything to have her. I snap from my fantasy and hurry toward the field.

Yes! Yes! Yes! That's it, baby. That's it!

Dust on her shirt, sweat on her face, she sees me, dressed to kill, on the sidelines.

"Need something cool?" I ask sweetly as I offer her a soft drink.

She nods her head and smiles.

Home run, for both of us.

Soccer

They dragged me to their impromptu soccer
game last Sunday morning. What I told them —
before they forced me out of the warmth of my
bed and into their car — is that I couldn't understand what a group of women were doing, up at
the crack of dawn, out in the cold, kicking a ball
across a wet field. Like I'm the only one who
went out Saturday night? Like I'm the only one
who wants to sleep in one lousy day a week?

I said no way. I work out at the gym three

times a week, I get my exercise there. But my buddies, playing on my well-known weakness for sporting events — okay, they hinted that Evelyn Anderson was known to ref these games — talked me into it.

Evelyn "the butch" Anderson . . . ? Shit, I figured I could sacrifice one Sunday morning for the good of the team. I said okay, one game, and one game only.

My damn alarm went on the blink Sunday and they showed up, pulling me out of bed at eight-fifteen. I barely had time to pull my hair into a pony tail.

"What point is there in playing when you don't look your best?" I complained dismally, thinking that perhaps a minor femme tantrum would buy me enough time to dampen and blow dry my hair.

Ginger tossed me shorts and a sweatshirt from my drawer as Kim pulled me away from the mirror. No one seemed interested in my perspective. Am I the only woman who understands the value of sexual distraction as a game strategy? Perplexed, I shook my head.

Within minutes, we were out of my apartment and piling into the car. As we raced over the bumpy back roads, I did my best to apply mascara and gloss. Things were going progressively downhill — hair in a pony tail, poor makeup lighting. I traced my lips with liner as best as I could and blotted them on Kim's matchbook cover.

I glanced one last time into the mirror. Eyes okay, lips looked full. All things considered, I could hold my own. Contemplating game strategy and the fact that a very hot Evelyn Anderson was calling the shots, I added a touch more blush. Well, if nothing else, at least I was looking out for the team.

We got to the field and stood around in the damp cold twenty minutes waiting for everyone to show. And worse than that, Evelyn Anderson was nowhere to be seen. Early Sunday morning and I'm standing in grass, out in the middle of nowhere, like I'm waiting for a goddamn bus.

Hell, I hadn't even had a chance to pee before they had hauled me out of bed and tossed me in the car. I headed toward the restrooms. Not paying much attention, I stepped in an unlocked stall, only to find myself face to face with none other than Evelyn Anderson.

"Oh, God, I'm sorry," I mumbled, embarrassed. "The door was unlocked . . . I thought it was . . ." I turned to exit the small booth.

From behind, Evelyn grabbed me by the sweatshirt and pulled me close. "Playing soccer today?" Her voice was a seductive whisper.

"Wha . . . well, yes," I stammered, caught off guard. My back was against her breasts. I didn't move.

"Wanna win?" She purred like a hungry cat. Her cold hand pushed beneath my sweatshirt.

I considered the team — the joy of winning, the agony of defeat. Of course we wanted to win. What kind of question was that for a sports-minded woman like myself? Evelyn's breath was hot on my neck, her hand only inches from my tingling nipples.

She tugged my ponytail. "Well, Ms. Soccer girl?"

Her hand slid toward my breasts and my heart began to pound.

"Yes," I muttered.

Evelyn pushed her fingers beneath my lace bra. My nipples hardened to tight points. She jammed her hands in my shorts and I was suddenly soaked with desire.

"C'mon," she urged. "All the way. All the way to goal."

She rooted me onward. Eyes closed, I raced, I flew, down the field — the ball was mine, the shot was mine, the glory was all mine. And her hand was relentless; her fingers nonstop.

"C'mon." She panted. "C'mon."

"Yeah." I moaned. And her fingers went on and on. She had me now. She had me good. "Yeah, yeah, yeah."

Whistles blew, the crowd roared. I was on my own — sweating, out of breath, faster, faster, faster. With the ref behind me all the way, I let it go with everything I had.

* * * * *

We won Sunday's game. Ginger and Kim were pretty impressed with my enthusiasm. In fact, they asked if I'd be interested in signing on this season with the bookstore team. I shook my head. After all, I could see Evelyn Saturday nights.

The Gym

Sure, I go to the gym. Sure, I work out. On the weight bench, wet with sweat — that's where you'll find me. Lift free weights? Leg curls and extensions? Not quite. After all, I'm a true sportswoman, I know the score.

Lie down, press hard and then get pumped. That *is* the idea, isn't it? Who needs three sets of twenty reps to accomplish that? Not me, not since Ace.

Ace works Thursday evenings. She trains the novices. Yeah, I'm a beginner — looking for a workout, looking to get wet. I walk in and sign up. My hot pink spandex outfit clings to my full curves and I can see a glimmer of approval in Ace's eyes.

Oh please, tell me you don't understand what I'm talking about. *Sure . . . we all wear spandex for maximum workout ease.* Yeah, right.

Only thinking of workout ease, I strut in skin-tight hot pink to the barbells. What a *big* surprise . . . Ace, most probably thinking how easy a student I'll be, is there in less than a spandex-snap second.

"So, how much experience you got?" she says, her voice as sultry as the summer night.

What do you say when a rock-hard butch asks a question like that? I glance at her bulging biceps, her thick thighs, her firm hands. *Plenty, baby.*

"Not much," I answer coyly.

She looks me up and down. "You lookin' to tighten up or build?"

I focus on her body-building fingers and murmur, "I guess I want to be tight."

"Gettin' women tight, that's my specialty," Ace says, attitude seeping from every pore.

That's when I start wondering why I had wasted so much goddamn time hanging around the baseball field the last month or so. Shit, when it comes to athletics, a smart sports enthusiast has to have her priorities straight.

"Got to warm you up first." Ace points to an exercycle. "Ten minutes."

I climb on the bike and start to pedal. Ace loses no time picking up a barbell and doing some reps. Standing before the full-length mirror, her muscles are firm, her stance steady, she looks good.

Beads of sweat tickle on my brow. One minute on the bike and I'm already sweating.

Ace tosses me a quick look. "You gettin' warm?"

"Yeah." I pant. I try to look nonchalant, like this goddamn bike is no big deal. Sweat starts seeping from under my arms. Perspiration on my brand new outfit, son of a bitch.

"This is a leg press," Ace says as she straddles a machine bench.

She's face up, legs bent in the air. From where I sit, I can almost see up her baggy gym shorts . . . and I thought spandex was the only way to go!

Was this bike set on uphill, or what? I'm drenched with sweat, pushing harder on the pedals and Ace lies, legs up and out, across from me.

"Works the thighs," she grunts as she extends her legs.

My sudden view up her shorts disappears. I

lean forward and pedal faster, as if somehow, if I hurry, I'd get a better peek.

Ace's legs resume their original, out and spread position. I'm whirling on the bike, racing along. Closer and closer. Yeah, if I look just right, if I angle just so, I'll see up those shorts — those wonderfully loose shorts.

My feet fly on the pedals. Sweat drips from my face. I'm so close I can almost see everything Ace has to offer. Her nipples stand erect beneath her thin white T-shirt. Her dark hair is plush under her panty-free gym shorts.

I make a sudden commitment to work out three, no four, no five times a week. Ace spreads her legs wider and, leaning over the handlebars, I zoom toward heaven. Oh shit, I can see everything. Faster, faster, I race alongside her.

C'mon, Ace. Keep them spread, Ace.

I grip the handlebars. I'll shoot through space if I let go.

Yeah, Ace. Yeah, Ace. Let me see it all.

I'm soaking wet. I'm sliding back and forth on the thick bicycle seat. *I'll work out every day, two times a day, three times a day — just don't move your legs, Ace.*

Out of nowhere a tiny bell rings. Ace climbs from the leg press and clicks off the exercycle timer.

"Good warmup, huh?" She runs her fingertip

across the sweat on my face then down my neck to my breast.

Yeah, I think I'm going to like getting pumped.

A Rising Star

I peer out the window at a rising star and the sudden urge to hurry to the bathroom overwhelms me. Airplanes are small. Airplanes are crowded. The man seated next to me is snoring. The woman next to him is engrossed in a magazine. Getting to the bathroom means climbing over them both.

"Excuse me, please."

He grunts and shifts in his seat. She gives me an annoyed frown.

"Sorry."

Down the aisle to the bathroom. One occupied. One vacant. Seconds later, I'm in. I glance at my reflection in the mirror. I'm a still-life black-and-white image huddled in the corner.

My black sport coat suggests class and sophistication. The new eyeliner enhances my dark eyes. I recall the women whose attraction to me was evident these past few days and in this bathroom, in this mirror, I try to see what they saw.

A fat tear wells on my eyelash and I'm careful not to move — unwilling to allow the eyeliner to run. There's comforting isolation in an airplane restroom. Alone, I search the mirror. I've rushed to the bathroom because an unexpected sadness shadowed a rising star. Will being locked in with myself help me find the sparkle?

Against my will, the tear races down my check and the liner smears. Will I ever feel brave enough to let someone touch my heart again? The place where past lovers touched has been closed for repair. Out of order. No trespassing. Do not disturb. Instead, I dream up fantasies. I close my eyes and spin a story, faster and faster, until tiny lights flicker in the gray.

A simple action, a single moment in time, alters until it glitters. I spin the fantasy until life seems safe and love, great.

Like last night. A simple action. A single moment.

Last night, after the workshop, a group of us went to dinner. An L.A. dinner party — a movie producer, the director, three stars from their film, a musician, a publisher, an editor and me — the editor's tag-along-story-writing friend. A round table, surrounded by beautiful women — clever women, high-powered women. I remember glancing around the table in a delighted daze.

The moment when the silver-haired butch across from me stood up, smiled and headed to the bathroom.

A simple action. A single moment. *A woman gets up from a table and smiles. A woman gets up from a table and smiles. A woman gets up from a table and smiles.*

If I had followed that silver-haired butch from the table?

The silver butch rises from the table. She crosses the room toward the bathroom. The moment spins, spins, spins — and I get up and follow her.

In the bathroom, we stand in front of the mirror, side by side. She sprinkles water on her fingers and runs them through her hair. I cream my lips with cherry-red lipstick and wonder if she likes what she sees.

She glances at me and I smile. *Like the lipstick? Like my curls? How about my eyes?* Seconds later, I'm in her arms. While our dinner companions finish their meals, while the waiter refills their water glasses — she kisses me. Over and over, she kisses me.

Kisses me.

Kisses me.

Is her name Bev or was Bev the one sitting next to her?

Bev was the one to her left. This silver-maned butch's name is ... ?

She has her hands up my skirt. She keeps muttering, "I wanted to fuck you from the moment I met you and all through dinner and while you were flirting with the woman to your right and —"

Has the movie director noticed our absence? Has the publisher turned to the editor and asked where we've gone? Is someone on their way to make sure we're okay?

And we are okay, aren't we? Her hand moving up my thigh — she's teasing the border of my panties with her finger. I'm all over her. How long since someone has taken me? How long since I've been touched?

Her finger slides beneath the lace and into the

spice. In less than a second — we're that close — a mere half an inch and she'd be between my lips and in my heat.

The worry that someone could come through the door is overshadowed by the delicious sensations her fingertip creates as it wiggles back and forth.

Come to think of it — who cares really about the door? It's as good as locked. After all, it's my fantasy — I can do what I please. No one gets in, unless I want them to. *Spin. Spin. Spin.*

Are they ordering dessert? Is the film producer curious why I'm not back at the table? After all, we'd talked up to that very moment when the silver-haired butch left the table.

Slick. Smooth as the silk suit she wore, the producer had eyed me all through appetizers. She was androgynous with a butch edge. Her black hair was a wispy shoulder length. She had a girlfriend, or so she said, but she flirted — all through dinner. I laughed. I sparkled. What harm was there to tease at a table for nine?

The airplane dips slightly and I grab the sink to steady myself. I glance in the mirror again . . .

What if the producer had gone to her car to retrieve her wallet? Instead of following the butch to the bathroom, what if I had slipped out after the producer? Would I have had the nerve to excuse myself? To say I needed a breath of fresh air?

Yes. I'd excuse myself and follow her to her car. I'm right behind her when she unlocks the door.

"I know you have a lover but —" I say, almost in a whisper. She turns to face me but says nothing. Have I insulted her or is that a flattered smile? It doesn't matter.

"You know I have a lover but —?" She seems sarcastic . . . or does she? God, I hate when my intuition is on the blink. She flirted with me at the table where it was safe. Where an out-of-town lover can do as she pleases. But now . . . now that we're alone, now that I've called her bluff . . .

A hurricane of ideas swirl around me. We'd simply climb in her car and do it in the back. Or maybe we'd go for a ride, get a suite in some fancy hotel, have room service bring us a table of desserts and sip an after-dinner aperitif.

With a woman like her, I'd wear only silk. With a woman like her, I'd wear only gold. With a woman like her, I'd feel as expensive as she looked.

We'd probably have to sneak into the back of her car. There isn't much time. In the restaurant, at the table, they are waiting for us. Is the silver butch eating double chocolate desire? Was Bev, to her left, sharing cheesecake with the musician?

In her car, the producer is on top of me. She has a way with words — hadn't she sweet-talked me, tempted me, flirted with me all through dinner? A woman like her could take me all sorts of places in the back of a car. I can see the promise of journey in her eyes. In the back of her car. In the back of her car.

In the back of her car, her fingers tease my mouth, my nipples, my belly. She could tease me all she wanted some other time, but for now, in the parking lot of a ritzy L.A. restaurant, we'd have to go fast.

"We could meet later tonight in my room." Her breath heats my ear as she speaks.

Yes. Her hotel . . . that would be good, but for now, I want to get acquainted. After all, weren't our dinner companions known to go on and on about business? Weren't they intently discussing the next big lesbian film?

Perhaps one of them should have been clever enough to bring along a video recorder. Hadn't they known that the next big star would be seated at their table? An untapped talent? Perhaps what could be happening out in that car would make the biggest lesbian film yet.

In that car, and short on time, I'd like her to go down on me. If she'd pull my panties aside and lace her tongue between my ample lips, I'd be pleased. When a woman sucks my clitoris into her mouth, on some secret level, I know she'll call again.

"We could meet later tonight in my room."

Had she thought I hadn't heard her the first

117

time? I knew about the room. I knew all about the possibilities of aperitifs and dessert but right now, in the back of the car, is where I want it — her fingers on my clit, her tongue burrowing into my slit, her teeth nipping at the opening.

She'd tug a sex lip with her fingers. Pull it. Stretch it. She'd give me everything I wanted and more. I'm the star. The leading lady. There are so many directions that we can go . . .

Perhaps if the director came looking for us — with her ebony hair and beady eyes, she'd know exactly what angles to shoot this scene. Would it be too crazy, too wild, too much to have her cross the lot in search of us?

From a director's point of view, attention would focus on panties pulled aside, fingers immersed in sugar-sweet pussy. She'd call for her camerawoman. Hell, she'd call for the entire crew.

In the back of a car, the rising star would close her eyes and let Hollywood do its thing.

In the back of a car. In the back of a car. In the back of a car.

The *fasten seat belt* sign rings. I glance in the mirror and in that moment, I can see what they saw — those women who looked at me with a sparkle in their eyes. I dab the smeared eyeliner from my cheek, click open the door and wander to my seat.

118

I peer out the window. The rising star has settled in the sky like a glittery, diamond pin. Three more stars flicker in the distance and home is just over the horizon.

In the Mood

How do I like it?
I want to be sweet-talked.
I want to feel safe.
I want to be swept up and carried away and all
   the while feel warm, warm, warm.
You tell me I'm pretty — I like that.
You tell me I'm sexy — I like that, too.

Your love seeps like glowing lava and swallows
   me, sucks the air from me, suffocates me.

That's fine. I'm ready. I want to drown in you.

"How do I like it?" you ask and I watch your
    mouth as you speak.
Your words hit like three shots of whiskey and
    I feel drunk.

With you, I'm spinning in a fantasy. A
    kaleidoscope of dreams. You lead. I follow. We
    don't talk about where we're going or where
    we've been. We don't have to — the path is
    clear.

I like to watch your mouth, did I mention that?
I like to watch your hands, have I told you that?
Have I told you how much I want you?
God, I ache for you — your sweet words
    whispered in my ear.
Your breathless kisses . . .

You ask me how I like it and I feel shy. You
    reassure me, you take care of me. You listen
    and ask me again and again.
"How do you like it?"
You want to please me —
I like that.

I believe in forever. With you. Forever. No one
    else. Never will be. Only you. You and me.
    That's how I like it . . .

... And your fingers and hands and kisses
    and lips ...
You make love to me, you fuck me — from fast
    to slow, hard to soft with fingers and kisses
    and words.
How do I like it?
The way you take me, want me, have me,
    cherish me, desire me, grab me, conquer me.
I call your name
and soar through the sky.
Wherever you go, take me, too.
That's how I like it and that's how it is.
I'm sweet for you. Crazy for you.
And in the mood.

MEETING MAGDALENE & OTHER STORIES by
Marilyn Freeman. 144 pp. Read the book, see the movie!
ISBN 1-56280-170-8   11.95

SECOND FIDDLE by Kate Calloway. 208 pp. P.I. Cassidy James'
second case.   ISBN 1-56280-169-6   11.95

LAUREL by Isabel Miller. 128 pp. By the author of the beloved
Patience and Sarah.   ISBN 1-56280-146-5   10.95

LOVE OR MONEY by Jackie Calhoun. 240 pp. The romance of
real life.   ISBN 1-56280-147-3   10.95

SMOKE AND MIRRORS by Pat Welch. 224 pp. 5th Helen Black
Mystery.   ISBN 1-56280-143-0   10.95

DANCING IN THE DARK edited by Barbara Grier & Christine
Cassidy. 272 pp. Erotic love stories by Naiad Press authors.
ISBN 1-56280-144-9   14.95

TIME AND TIME AGAIN by Catherine Ennis. 176 pp. Passionate
love affair.   ISBN 1-56280-145-7   10.95

PAXTON COURT by Diane Salvatore. 256 pp. Erotic and wickedly
funny contemporary tale about the business of learning to live
together.   ISBN 1-56280-114-7   10.95

INNER CIRCLE by Claire McNab. 208 pp. 8th Carol Ashton
Mystery.   ISBN 1-56280-135-X   10.95

LESBIAN SEX: AN ORAL HISTORY by Susan Johnson.
240 pp. Need we say more?   ISBN 1-56280-142-2   14.95

BABY, IT'S COLD by Jaye Maiman. 256 pp. 5th Robin Miller
Mystery.   ISBN 1-56280-141-4   19.95

WILD THINGS by Karin Kallmaker. 240 pp. By the undisputed
mistress of lesbian romance.   ISBN 1-56280-139-2   10.95

THE GIRL NEXT DOOR by Mindy Kaplan. 208 pp. Just what
you'd expect.   ISBN 1-56280-140-6   11.95

NOW AND THEN by Penny Hayes. 240 pp. Romance on the
westward journey.   ISBN 1-56280-121-X   11.95

HEART ON FIRE by Diana Simmonds. 176 pp. The romantic and
erotic rival of *Curious Wine.*   ISBN 1-56280-152-X   11.95

DEATH AT LAVENDER BAY by Lauren Wright Douglas. 208 pp.
1st Allison O'Neil Mystery.   ISBN 1-56280-085-X   11.95

YES I SAID YES I WILL by Judith McDaniel. 272 pp. Hot
romance by famous author.   ISBN 1-56280-138-4   11.95

FORBIDDEN FIRES by Margaret C. Anderson. Edited by Mathilda
Hills. 176 pp. Famous author's "unpublished" Lesbian romance.
ISBN 1-56280-123-6   21.95

SIDE TRACKS by Teresa Stores. 160 pp. Gender-bending
Lesbians on the road.   ISBN 1-56280-122-8   10.95

HOODED MURDER by Annette Van Dyke. 176 pp. 1st Jessie
Batelle Mystery.   ISBN 1-56280-134-1   10.95

WILDWOOD FLOWERS by Julia Watts. 208 pp. Hilarious and
heart-warming tale of true love.   ISBN 1-56280-127-9   10.95

NEVER SAY NEVER by Linda Hill. 224 pp. Rule #1: Never get involved
with . . .   ISBN 1-56280-126-0   10.95

THE SEARCH by Melanie McAllester. 240 pp. Exciting top cop
Tenny Mendoza case.   ISBN 1-56280-150-3   10.95

THE WISH LIST by Saxon Bennett. 192 pp. Romance through
the years.   ISBN 1-56280-125-2   10.95

FIRST IMPRESSIONS by Kate Calloway. 208 pp. P.I. Cassidy
James' first case.   ISBN 1-56280-133-3   10.95

OUT OF THE NIGHT by Kris Bruyer. 192 pp. Spine-tingling
thriller.   ISBN 1-56280-120-1   10.95

NORTHERN BLUE by Tracey Richardson. 224 pp. Police recruits
Miki & Miranda — passion in the line of fire.   ISBN 1-56280-118-X   10.95

LOVE'S HARVEST by Peggy J. Herring. 176 pp. by the author of
Once More With Feeling.   ISBN 1-56280-117-1   10.95

THE COLOR OF WINTER by Lisa Shapiro. 208 pp. Romantic
love beyond your wildest dreams.   ISBN 1-56280-116-3   10.95

FAMILY SECRETS by Laura DeHart Young. 208 pp. Enthralling
romance and suspense.   ISBN 1-56280-119-8   10.95

INLAND PASSAGE by Jane Rule. 288 pp. Tales exploring conven-
tional & unconventional relationships.   ISBN 0-930044-56-8   10.95

DOUBLE BLUFF by Claire McNab. 208 pp. 7th Carol Ashton
Mystery.   ISBN 1-56280-096-5   10.95

BAR GIRLS by Lauran Hoffman. 176 pp. See the movie, read
the book!   ISBN 1-56280-115-5   10.95

THE FIRST TIME EVER edited by Barbara Grier & Christine
Cassidy. 272 pp. Love stories by Naiad Press authors.
                                           ISBN 1-56280-086-8   14.95

MISS PETTIBONE AND MISS McGRAW by Brenda Weathers.
208 pp. A charming ghostly love story.   ISBN 1-56280-151-1   10.95

CHANGES by Jackie Calhoun. 208 pp. Involved romance and
relationships.   ISBN 1-56280-083-3   10.95

FAIR PLAY by Rose Beecham. 256 pp. 3rd Amanda Valentine
Mystery.   ISBN 1-56280-081-7   10.95

PAYBACK by Celia Cohen. 176 pp. A gripping thriller of romance,
revenge and betrayal.   ISBN 1-56280-084-1   10.95

THE BEACH AFFAIR by Barbara Johnson. 224 pp. Sizzling
summer romance/mystery/intrigue.   ISBN 1-56280-090-6   10.95

GETTING THERE by Robbi Sommers. 192 pp. Nobody does it
like Robbi! ISBN 1-56280-099-X 10.95

FINAL CUT by Lisa Haddock. 208 pp. 2nd Carmen Ramirez
Mystery. ISBN 1-56280-088-4 10.95

FLASHPOINT by Katherine V. Forrest. 256 pp. A Lesbian
blockbuster! ISBN 1-56280-079-5 11.95

CLAIRE OF THE MOON by Nicole Conn. Audio Book —Read
by Marianne Hyatt. ISBN 1-56280-113-9 16.95

FOR LOVE AND FOR LIFE: INTIMATE PORTRAITS OF
LESBIAN COUPLES by Susan Johnson. 224 pp.
ISBN 1-56280-091-4 14.95

DEVOTION by Mindy Kaplan. 192 pp. See the movie — read
the book! ISBN 1-56280-093-0 10.95

SOMEONE TO WATCH by Jaye Maiman. 272 pp. 4th Robin
Miller Mystery. ISBN 1-56280-095-7 10.95

GREENER THAN GRASS by Jennifer Fulton. 208 pp. A young
woman — a stranger in her bed. ISBN 1-56280-092-2 10.95

TRAVELS WITH DIANA HUNTER by Regine Sands. Erotic
lesbian romp. Audio Book (2 cassettes) ISBN 1-56280-107-4 16.95

CABIN FEVER by Carol Schmidt. 256 pp. Sizzling suspense
and passion. ISBN 1-56280-089-1 10.95

THERE WILL BE NO GOODBYES by Laura DeHart Young. 192
pp. Romantic love, strength, and friendship. ISBN 1-56280-103-1 10.95

FAULTLINE by Sheila Ortiz Taylor. 144 pp. Joyous comic
lesbian novel. ISBN 1-56280-108-2 9.95

OPEN HOUSE by Pat Welch. 176 pp. 4th Helen Black Mystery.
ISBN 1-56280-102-3 10.95

ONCE MORE WITH FEELING by Peggy J. Herring. 240 pp.
Lighthearted, loving romantic adventure. ISBN 1-56280-089-2 11.95

FOREVER by Evelyn Kennedy. 224 pp. Passionate romance — love
overcoming all obstacles. ISBN 1-56280-094-9 10.95

WHISPERS by Kris Bruyer. 176 pp. Romantic ghost story
ISBN 1-56280-082-5 10.95

NIGHT SONGS by Penny Mickelbury. 224 pp. 2nd Gianna Maglione
Mystery. ISBN 1-56280-097-3 10.95

GETTING TO THE POINT by Teresa Stores. 256 pp. Classic
southern Lesbian novel. ISBN 1-56280-100-7 10.95

PAINTED MOON by Karin Kallmaker. 224 pp. Delicious
Kallmaker romance. ISBN 1-56280-075-2 11.95

THE MYSTERIOUS NAIAD edited by Katherine V. Forrest &
Barbara Grier. 320 pp. Love stories by Naiad Press authors.
ISBN 1-56280-074-4 14.95

DAUGHTERS OF A CORAL DAWN by Katherine V. Forrest.
240 pp. Tenth Anniversay Edition.   ISBN 1-56280-104-X   11.95

BODY GUARD by Claire McNab. 208 pp. 6th Carol Ashton
Mystery.   ISBN 1-56280-073-6   11.95

CACTUS LOVE by Lee Lynch. 192 pp. Stories by the beloved
storyteller.   ISBN 1-56280-071-X   9.95

SECOND GUESS by Rose Beecham. 216 pp. 2nd Amanda Valentine
Mystery.   ISBN 1-56280-069-8   9.95

A RAGE OF MAIDENS by Lauren Wright Douglas. 240 pp. 6th Caitlin
Reece Mystery.   ISBN 1-56280-068-X   10.95

TRIPLE EXPOSURE by Jackie Calhoun. 224 pp. Romantic drama
involving many characters.   ISBN 1-56280-067-1   10.95

UP, UP AND AWAY by Catherine Ennis. 192 pp. Delightful
romance.   ISBN 1-56280-065-5   11.95

PERSONAL ADS by Robbi Sommers. 176 pp. Sizzling short
stories.   ISBN 1-56280-059-0   11.95

CROSSWORDS by Penny Sumner. 256 pp. 2nd Victoria Cross
Mystery.   ISBN 1-56280-064-7   9.95

SWEET CHERRY WINE by Carol Schmidt. 224 pp. A novel of
suspense.   ISBN 1-56280-063-9   9.95

CERTAIN SMILES by Dorothy Tell. 160 pp. Erotic short stories.
    ISBN 1-56280-066-3   9.95

EDITED OUT by Lisa Haddock. 224 pp. 1st Carmen Ramirez
Mystery.   ISBN 1-56280-077-9   9.95

WEDNESDAY NIGHTS by Camarin Grae. 288 pp. Sexy
adventure.   ISBN 1-56280-060-4   10.95

SMOKEY O by Celia Cohen. 176 pp. Relationships on the
playing field.   ISBN 1-56280-057-4   9.95

KATHLEEN O'DONALD by Penny Hayes. 256 pp. Rose and
Kathleen find each other and employment in 1909 NYC.
    ISBN 1-56280-070-1   9.95

STAYING HOME by Elisabeth Nonas. 256 pp. Molly and Alix
want a baby . . . or do they?   ISBN 1-56280-076-0   10.95

TRUE LOVE by Jennifer Fulton. 240 pp. Six lesbians searching
for love in all the "right" places.   ISBN 1-56280-035-3   10.95